BOMBAY BALCHÃO

Jane Borges is a Mumbai-based journalist. She currently writes on books, heritage and urban planning for *Sunday mid-day*, the weekend edition of the *mid-day* newspaper. She has previously co-authored *Mafia Queens of Mumbai: Stories of Women from the Ganglands* with S. Hussain Zaidi in 2011.

D1645188

9030 00006 3342 1

Praise for *Bombay Balchão*

'*Bombay Balchão*, rich in detail about the customs, costumes and culinary traditions of Goans and Mangaloreans in Bombay is a love letter by the author to a neighbourhood mostly forgotten.'

—*India Today*

'Suffused by a sense of romanticism triggered by a patch of land, *Bombay Balchão* belongs in the company of works such as Nalini Jones' *What You Call Winter*, Rohinton Mistry's *Tales from Firozeshah Baag* and VS Naipaul's *Miguel Street*.'

—*Open*

'Borges's novel seems to be a carefully disguised bildungsroman that collates history and memory into a celebration of the joy of storytelling.'

—*The Telegraph*

'Wrapped in the noise and crowd of Mumbai, a little slice of Goa reaches out to you through these stories.'

—*Outlook Traveller*

'Above the gripping plot lines, this maiden fiction effort is really about the charms of an old city with a rich past, lost to today's nuclear, concrete Mumbai.'

—*The Hindu Literary Review*

'Borges takes the concept of the pickle recipe and turns it into a metaphor for living.'

—*Asian Review of Books*

'Given that one of the macro trends that a fair bit of Bombay-writing falls into is the maximum city extravaganza, of crime or politics or the grand drama of poetry and drugs, *Bombay Balchão* situates itself in the quietly resistant strain of the domestic novel that, like Anjali Joseph's *Saraswati Park* or Amrita Mahale's *Milk Teeth*, allows the richly detailed specificity of a particular world to tell eloquently of the inner life of the metropolis just as well if not better than their more OTT versions.'

—*The Asian Age*

'There is passion, enmity, hatred, disappointment, ambition: all the emotions that make up human life. Borges tells her story well and with an empathy that one cannot help but warm to.'

—*The New Indian Express*

KU-603-031

BOMBAY BALCHÃO

JANE BORGES

First published in hardback in 2019 by Tranquebar, an imprint of Westland Publications Private Limited

First published in paperback in 2021 by Tranquebar, an imprint of Westland Publications Private Limited

1st Floor, A Block, East Wing, Plot No. 40, SP Infocity, Dr MGR Salai, Perungudi, Kandanchavadi, Chennai 600096

Westland, the Westland logo, Tranquebar and the Tranquebar logo are the trademarks of Westland Publications Private Limited, or its affiliates.

Copyright © Jane Borges, 2019

Jane Borges asserts the moral right to be identified as the author of this work.

ISBN: 9789389152081

10 9 8 7 6 5 4 3 2 1

This is a work of fiction. Names, characters, organisations, places, events and incidents are either products of the author's imagination or used fictitiously.

All rights reserved

Book design by Jojy Philip, New Delhi 110 015

Printed at Thomson Press (India) Ltd

No part of this book may be reproduced, or stored in a retrieval system, or transmitted in any form or by any means, electronic, mechanical, photocopying, recording, or otherwise, without express written permission of the publisher.

To Dada, Mamma and
my brothers, Saby and Steven.
Thank you for the gift of family.

CONTENTS

1

PAPER HEARTS

December 2015

We never saw snowflakes on Christmas. Not in my neighbourhood at least. Even if they were to fall from our winter sky, they'd melt into drops of dew, nervously resting on pink-petalled flowers. Yet, each year, when the cold months set in, we'd secretly wish for a white Christmas so that we could build ourselves a portly snowman with button eyes and a carrot nose. But that sweltering December from seventy years ago dashed any such hopes.

Before we begin, you must know where you are. Sandwiched between two bustling bazaars in the south of Mumbai is a winding stretch of road, broken on the edges and pockmarked from years of neglect. From dawn to twilight, hurried feet trample over this uneven strip, while handcarts crush and pound it further, making its presence unsightly. At the mouth of the lane, hanging perilously from a wrought iron pole is a plaque the colour of midnight blue. The inconspicuous sans serif font in waning white reads: Dr D'Lima Street, Cavel.

Back in 1945, there was no signboard to welcome you. There was instead, a dirt track that opened into our street, dotted by villas and surrounded by gulmohar and chiku trees.

Winter evenings here were always cold and pleasant, if not biting. The raucous hawkers who lined our street would escape early to avoid the nip, and those who stayed built a fire to keep themselves warm. This is why the Christmas Eve from that year stood out like a sore thumb. The light mist that would otherwise float aimlessly under the incandescent glow of the streetlights had not made an appearance. Neither had the shimmering constellation—Orion, a result of stars crisscrossing to create a bow-and-arrow wielding hunter, had been shadowed by a flock of dark, grey clouds. It was a strange night, compounded by stranger happenings inside our church.

The four-hundred-odd parishioners of Our Lady of Hope, who between carolling and prayer had witnessed one of these incidents, would remember it to their dying breath. For years to come, the tale would be discussed at every social gathering in Cavel, often laced with Goan recheado and balchão masala. It wasn't long before the marinated apocrypha began to vary from household to household. The characters and plot changed with every story, but the residents of Cavel continued to listen to it with the same curiosity and anticipation with which they had heard it the first time around.

I never felt the need to contribute to these stories. Mine would only meld into this clutter, and I did not want that to happen. There was another reason. Not only did I have an entirely different account of the incident that set the rumour mills turning, I had also been witness to something that I had deliberately never spoken about. For some reason, I buried this part of my life so deep that even if I wanted to summon it, the memory would be so hazy that it wouldn't cause me an ounce of pain.

Our minds are surprisingly gifted with this innate ability to omit events that we do not to wish to revisit. But a slight trigger and the mind retrieves them for us, playing them out in technicolour.

The weather tonight is so much like it was that night in 1945 that the very thought hurts my heart. The air is withdrawn and the clouds heavy just like that day when I—a gangly-looking, awkward teenager of fourteen—sat in church as Fr Augustine Fernandez led the midnight mass.

Cavel had its own swing during this season, drawing residents into crazy merriment. The houses in our lane would be lit up with candles, and even the trees abutting them were decorated to shine like the sun. After midnight mass, everyone would throng the compound below my building, 193-A, Bosco Mansion at Pope's Colony, for a Christmas party that saw revellers arrive from as far as Mahim, the last stop of the island city before Bombay spilt into the suburbs. Each parishioner had unspoken duties here. While the boys would take care of the bonfire, burning logs of deadwood and stacks of hay picked up from the nearby Crawford Market to light up the grounds, the older men would be immersed in creating potent concoctions of home-brewed alcohol that would be served only after the night got younger. The women, on the other hand, would play kind hosts, first feeding the famished coffee and plum cakes before tempting them with the more delicious mutton and pork chops. But what they all contributed to separately, they compensated together in celebration as they flirted and danced and even broke into solemn singing—the home favourites being *Silent Night* and *Hark the Herald Angels Sing*—leaving only after the sun had ambushed the dark so that they could prepare for the feasting in their homes through Christmas Day.

On that night too, a get-together had been planned. And so, hoping in earnest that the weather would not prick our happy bubble, we tried to put our best foot forward. By 11.30 p.m., most of the homes on the street had been abandoned. The click-clack of heavily heeled boots could be heard on the stretch—usually noiseless at that hour—as the men and women made a beeline to church for midnight mass.

My mother had got Francis, the tailor from John D'souza & Sons, to make her a long yellow silk gown, which swept the road as she walked to church. Her gold-laced mantilla, a head covering worn by the women, compulsorily for mass, hid her heavily powdered face and the crimson lips that she had painted with cheap lipstick, and my father was grateful for that. She looked ugly in make-up, he felt, but he could never muster the courage to tell her. He'd rather shut up than incur her stony silence once she'd been told.

Meanwhile, the Hindus, only a handful on our street, sneakily peered from the gaps between the iron rods of their windows, gawking at the dressy Christian women. It was an annual ritual. This was a time when even the radio was a rarity and people sought entertainment in the most bizarre places.

As members of the Hindu family gathered at the windowsill and gaped in awe, the patriarch of the house would break into the much-anticipated spiel about the 'converts' who had sold their souls to the gori chamdi. Their brazen act of aping the

Europeans at a time when freedom fighters were warring against the 'gore log' for independence and demanding that their brethren wear only hand-spun Indian cloth clearly showed which side of the battle the Christians were on, he argued.

'Mark my words, when the time arrives, they will be the first ones to leave with their sahibs and memsahibs. And if they don't, we'll drive them away.'

But the male libido had been sparked. In the darkness, numbed by furious lovemaking, he would latch onto his wife's waist, and in between suckling her breasts ask if she would wear one of those dresses, just for him. She would agree coyly, but as an afterthought dredge up the same repulsed feeling her husband had exposed in front of the family when he saw the Christian women strut on the roads. Was that how he would feel when he saw his wife in a dress? She couldn't tell.

At Our Lady of Hope, the crowd was slowly thickening. The church had once been the private chapel of a Portuguese merchant named Benito Pedro De Moura. He built it not very far from the temple of Mumbadevi, the Goddess the city owes its name to. It was a simple structure of stone with a lofty wooden roof which no man—at least, that's what we kids were told—could reach without the help of God. The rectangular nave, which boasted intricate, hand-made floral patterns on its red-oxide flooring, could accommodate a congregation of not more than three hundred people. Fortunately, since Cavel delivered more choristers than babies, every year for whom separate seating arrangements were made on a sturdy balcony right above the entrance, everyone was assured room.

But humidity levels spiralled inside the church that day, making it uncomfortable for everyone. To allow the heat to swim out, the huge arched windows had been left wide open, but there was still no respite. The ladies saw this as the perfect occasion to bring out the cloth fans they had been desperately waiting to flaunt since after summer. The striking paintings of lands unknown on their fans notwithstanding, their eyes still wore the glint of envy as they observed with awe the handiwork of different tailors on other women. The richer among them had come in gowns embroidered with sequins and accessorised with rows of gold necklaces encrusted with coral or pearl. It was as if they had emptied their jewellery boxes to flaunt their family wealth when the church always harped about frugality. The men who had come in three-piece hand-me-down suits that had long fallen out of favour with fashion, settled for their kerchiefs or made do with the faint warm air that passed their sides as their wives and daughters fanned their own faces. They were distracted too, but only the bachelors seated right at the back dared to make a show of their roving eyes.

Standing in front on a semi-circular raised pulpit, facing the altar and leading this pack into prayer was Fr Augustine Fernandez, whose white vestment glowed in the light of a candle chandelier, making him appear the most hallowed within this sea of humanity. Having served him in close and unsecure quarters as an altar boy, I found something comical about his personality. Always fidgety and nervous, with his round face bobbing on his short and portly body like that of a a Kuchipudi dancing doll, Fr Augustine's demeanour forever perplexed me. Everyone else, however, including my own family, was smitten by him and described his reticent nature as the trait of a true servant of God.

The uncomfortable weather seemed to have aggravated his anxiety, especially while he was reading the Gospel of Luke from the Bible. Part of the mass was in Latin, the language of the Gods, which only a few understood. But I, for long, had been a keen student of Latin, and on the insistence of my father, was being schooled separately in order to read and learn the Bible. It was how I realised that Fr Augustine wasn't focussing; something about the passage he was reading didn't sound quite right.

The place where he stood was indeed a furnace, and the huge candle that had been strategically placed near the pulpit wasn't doing him any good. He continued reading, occasionally wiping the beads of sweat that brushed his lips.

This was just the build-up to the drama that was to unfold. Because, five minutes later, when Fr Augustine had completed the gospel and had moved his hands upwards to join his palms in prayer, the elbow of his left arm accidentally hit the candle beside him. The wax cylinder dropped onto the floor, but not before lighting up the back of the gold-embroidered chasuble which he wore over his vestment.

'Fr Augustine is on fire,' a man screamed from among the crowd. The congregation was suddenly alerted. The priest himself wasn't aware of the fire, but the cries of the man who had alarmed him and the others had been so petrifying that, without thinking, he hurried down the steps of the pulpit and rushed towards the backyard garden, where a water tank was located. The churchgoers scurried after him; the collective clicking of their shoes on the floor left a loud and disturbing echo in the church.

To Fr Augustine's luck, his escape had been greeted with a blast of thunder. By the time he reached the water tank, the clouds had torn apart, exploding into a heavy shower that instantly doused his burning chasuble. 'December rain,' somebody yelled. 'This is a miracle. This is God's Christmas miracle.'

For the many hundreds of parishioners who had followed their beloved Fr Augustine in a bid to save him, the rain was indeed a blessing. The men snuggled their priest in a warm embrace. The rest broke out in prayer and someone started the opening lines of a rosary as the downpour continued.

'God cast out the devil that had tried to attack his servant,' is what they would later make of the incident.

Nobody, not even the priest, realised that it was just a few centimetres of the thin satin lining of his chasuble that had attracted the flames.

But just like that, this story from Christmas Eve came to be regarded as a legend in the Catholic neighbourhood of Cavel. The last story I heard spelt out in detail how Fr Augustine resembled a ball of flame when he ran out of the church, his arms flailing as if begging for succour. No one wanted to know how he had escaped the incident unscathed and went on to live for another thirty-six years, ripening till eighty, without marks of the burns that had sent him scampering like a mad man. Fr Augustine remained mum about the incident. The ludicrous stories that did the rounds soon after would trouble him throughout his life.

When I met him a few years after he left our parish, he admitted he was guilty of not having shut down those rambling stories. 'I wasn't sure what happened,' he confessed.

He, however, claimed to have figured out why he had been handpicked for this public humiliation. 'I haven't told this to anyone, son,' he whispered. I guided my ears to listen to him, wondering if there was another side to this story and if he had been the victim of some foul play. 'The sweat had glazed my eyes,' he said hesitantly. 'I ... I ... I don't know how I skipped the two most important passages of the gospel during the reading.'

A prolonged silence followed before he muttered, 'I distorted God's word. I was the devil. I had to be punished.'

As he said this, he heaved a sigh of relief, grateful that he had finally unburdened himself. I looked at him with pity but chuckled inwardly, resisting the urge to laugh out loud. God would have too.

While this tale enshrined itself in the collective receding memory of my neighbourhood, another one, which occurred on the same night and at the same place, was forgotten. In the beginning, it would affect me no end to think that an entire bunch of people had conveniently chosen to erase the incident from their minds, and all for a miracle that never really was. Yet, the more I thought about it, the more I realised that some lies are often only said so that a few truths are concealed. The bigger the lie, the more painful the truth.

The second incident took place right after the congregation had started the rosary near the tank. While I had joined the crowd, my mother had sent me back inside to be with my grandmother Maria Lorna Coutinho, who was having trouble with her joints. I was meant to watch over her, but shamai, as we fondly called her, was not one to spare herself all the fun. When I told her of the prayer that had begun outside, she shut her eyes and started mumbling the rosary too.

Apart from shamai's frantic lip movements, it was peaceful in here. The walls of the church blocked off the commotion outside, and I liked it that way. From the looks of it, the midnight service wouldn't resume anytime soon. Disinterested and sleepy, I rested my head on the top rail of the pew to catch a quick nap when someone whispered into my ear, 'Michael.'

The soft timbre of her voice had a soothing effect on me. Instead of waking me up, it pushed me deeper into the crevices of a beautiful dream.

When this person called out to me again—this time, a few decibels louder—an odd sensation kicked in and stirred me out of my slumber. That's when I realised I wasn't dreaming. My eyes opened to stare right into hers, even as my lips nervously curled into a sheepish smile, leaving two tiny depressions on either cheek.

Tracey, who was born the same year as me and was my ground-floor neighbour at Bosco Mansion, had been sitting several rows behind me, somewhere at the far corner of the church. I hadn't noticed that she had not gone with her mother to join the parishioners outside. This was not something I should have missed. In fact, she was the only reason I came to church. The one advantage of being an altar server, whose tasks involved assisting the priest with the mass proceedings, was that you got a ringside view of the crowd. Standing there, I always looked for Tracey. Now that I no longer served, combing through the crowd for her took a bit more effort, but it was still worth it.

The first time I met Tracey was when we were five years old. She had dressed as a flower girl during a celebration at church that we called the Eucharistic Adoration, which, in our church, went on for thirteen hours at a stretch. On this day, Christians from every street in Cavel would take turns venerating the Holy Eucharist that comprised the bread and wine symbolic of Jesus' body and blood. In the final hour, the Eucharist would be taken in a grand procession led by the parish priest, of parishioners and a musical band, from the church to the ground at Pope's Colony—the compound served the dual purpose of party and prayer ground—and later back to the church. Sweet, sweet Tracey was part of this procession, swaying in a pretty white dress and red velvet sash, dropping the rose petals she carried with her in a straw basket. There was a certain delicateness to how she let those petals fall—she only picked one petal each time, never holding them together in a bunch like other girls—tossing it gently to the ground. I had been standing right beside her, but I am not sure if we spoke.

A year later, when Tracey's family moved into our building, she would join me and my other friends, including Ellena Gomes and the da Cunha boys from the neighbouring Lobo Mansion, to play hopscotch and hide-and-seek. But Tracey loved the games we played on rainy days the most, and if I didn't show up, she'd knock on our door and beg mother to allow me to come down with her.

'Aunty, aunty, Michael promised to sail paper boats with me. Please let him come,' she'd say. My mother would agree, though reluctantly. She knew that I would catch a fever soon after, but 'if the rains bring you both closer,' she'd tell me, 'let the fever be the sacrifice.'

'Lady, stop messing with my son's head,' my father, Alfred Coutinho, would butt in. 'The D'Lima queen would never allow such a union. Over her dead body.'

But you couldn't tell mama to choose her dreams wisely.

You see, Tracey's grandfather, the venerable Dr Ralph Norman D'Lima, son of Goan educator Norman D'Lima, was among those who fell just short of having a shrine in his memory. Until the late 1930s, the D'Limas owned a bungalow on a sprawling expanse of land that boasted, among many other things, a dairy farm. When Norman wasn't teaching English and arithmetic at the fledgeling Catholic School run by the Society of Jesus in the same lane, he was busy milking his cows. It wasn't long before Gaiwadi, as his farm was called, started supplying milk to all and sundry, making this passion enterprise a hit. But it was his son, Dr Ralph, who changed the fortunes of the family. Tales of his compassion for the sickly were told to children as bedtime stories.

Dr Ralph was our local hero, just like Dr Acacio Gabriel Viegas, the celebrated doctor from the neighbouring Dhobi Talao area, whose resplendent statue outside the Parsi library, Cowasji Framjee Hall (though fallen into neglect today with pigeon droppings sullying him from head to toe) has forever made Goans gloat with pride. When Bombay was diseased with the bubonic plague of 1896, it was Dr Viegas who had stemmed the burgeoning death toll by detecting the first case in Mandvi. From there on, he doggedly spearheaded the movement to fight the epidemic, personally inoculating over eighteen thousand residents. His efforts eventually secured him the prized presidential berth in the Bombay Municipal Corporation. His contemporaries, including Dr D'Lima, had also helped see the plague through. They later took a leaf out of his phenomenal legacy and worked towards uplifting the city's health scene in the early 1900s. Efforts were made to convince the Bombay municipality to install a stone bust of Dr D'Lima at the mouth of our street, which led into Cavel. But as a piecemeal offering, the nameless road where his family resided was renamed Dr D'Lima Street nearly a decade after his death in 1939.

Mama never let a day go by without reminding me of how Dr D'Lima had fought tooth and nail to save her grandfather, Antao D'Costa, who had also been a victim of the plague. 'He died in the arms of Dr D'Lima. It was such a good death,' she claimed.

Dr D'Lima's daughter-in-law Linda Mary, on the other hand, was Cavel's anti-hero. She did not let go of any opportunity to remind her neighbours that she belonged to the crème de la crème of the Goan community. After a financial crisis, when the family was forced to tear down the D'Lima bungalow and move lock, stock and barrel to our building, Linda was said to have been most ruffled by the turn of events. Having lost her privacy, both inside—she no longer had her own piano room—and outside, she had become peevish and restless. She mostly kept to herself and never once indulged in empty conversations with the residents of Pope's Colony. The only time she spoke to my mother was to reprimand her when she thought I had kissed her daughter Tracey. 'Keep his filthy lips off my daughter's,' she had warned after she had seen Tracey scribble something in her maths book. 'Michael + Tracey = Kiss,' she had written.

'Is this what you teach your son, Mrs Coutinho?' Linda had asked mother.

My mother was unaffected. In fact, she considered it a personal victory and later gave me a chocolate bar for hastening her plans to make me the son-in-law of such an illustrious family.

'But I didn't kiss her,' I clarified.

'Aye, son, let Lady Linda believe you did, men,' she said.

After that incident, I saw very little of Tracey except during the monsoon when her mother escaped for a break to her hometown in Goa. That's when her father, an architect and a lovely soul just like Dr D'Lima, allowed her to play with me.

I have fond memories of those days. When the rain splattered into our compound and was no longer welcomed by the ever-relenting and absorbing earth, it broke into tiny, snaky rivulets that sought no direction or home. We sailed paper boats in these streams, and Tracey always won. My boat would drown mid-way somewhere, causing her to break into peals of laughter.

'Loser!' she'd say. I said nothing in response. All I did was muster a stupid smile which I knew kept her from teasing me further. But she'd get so nervous that she'd quickly add, 'Stop smiling, will you? I hate that smile.'

She couldn't even lie with a straight face.

Once her mother returned, Tracey and I behaved like we didn't know each other. When our eyes locked briefly in church during Sunday service, she'd put her head down immediately. Whom were we appeasing? Linda, I presume.

A year before that Christmas, everything stopped. Tracey no longer came to sail paper boats with me. In fact, she barely came out of her home. She'd come to church occasionally and when that happened, I would be overjoyed. Unfortunately, I saw no signs of similar happiness on her face. Our chance meetings got rarer by the day, until that Christmas Eve, when she came to mass in a lime-coloured frock. Though I had not seen her in months, my heart skipped a beat. But in the aftermath of the chaos, I had briefly overlooked her presence.

'Tracey,' I said now, as she stood next to me. I was trying hard to keep a straight face, even though my tiny dimples and reddened cheeks gave too much away. It would be a lie if I said my heart wasn't racing when she called out to me. I was also sweating profusely, but I wouldn't want to romanticise that part, because it had a lot to do with the heat.

'Hello,' I stammered.

'Can I sit here?' she asked, seemingly short of breath.

I threw a glance at shamai and seeing her still immersed in prayer, softly responded, 'Of course.'

She sat down at once beside me—there was a distance of just a few inches between us. It was only when Tracey was close enough that I noticed how pale she had become. Her cheeks were sunken, and her once gleaming eyes now wore the dullness of poor health. Her hands too had shrivelled. She was all skin and bone.

'Are you well?' I asked.

'Why do you ask?' Her voice had also thinned.

'No, no, just,' I lied. 'Where have you been? I hardly see you around these days.'

'Does it matter? You never came looking for me anyway.'

Even in her teasing, I could sense the tone of accusation. 'I didn't know where you were.'

'Don't lie, Michael,' she said, cutting me off. 'You could have just asked dada. He would have told you. But you never even came.' She spoke haltingly, as if measuring her words.

'How do you know?' I asked.

'Dada told me,' she said, sounding hurt.

I wish I had the courage to tell her that she was wrong. But when you love someone dearly, you allow their truth to take precedence over yours.

My truth was very different from hers. I had gone once too often to her home to enquire after her, only to be shooed away by both her parents, right at the door. Her father, in particular, had been ignoring me, choosing not to respond even to plain greetings when our paths crossed in the compound. When my mother learnt of it, she was so livid that she warned me against going there again. It was then that I started dropping letters into the mailbox at Tracey's door—at last count, ten—but all of them went unanswered. One day, out of sheer desperation, I even did my school homework on the steps of her ground-floor home, sitting there till dusk in the hope that she'd appear in front of me. Had I shared all of this with Tracey then, she'd have been disappointed and hurt with her parents—the people she most trusted. How could I have let that happen? And so, instead of responding or reacting to the lies, I just sat quietly with her, staring vacantly at the altar.

'I think I am very ill,' she finally said, breaking the silence between us.

I looked at her uncertainly, wondering if she was teasing me again.

'The doctors told me I have tuberculosis,' she said. I was shocked of course, but I don't remember showing any sign of that. By now, shamai was on the final part of her rosary, far too engrossed to even be rattled by what Tracey had just said.

'Are you better now?'

'I think so. I have stopped coughing at least,' she said. 'You know where I was all this time?'

'At home?'

'No.'

'Then?'

'I was kept in a special room at a hospital. I was all alone,' she said, speaking slowly.

'Why?'

'Because my parents didn't want me to die.'

In those days, tuberculosis was far deadlier than it is now. Patients were quarantined in open-air sanatoriums outside the city to prevent the rapid spread of the infection. It made sense that Tracey's parents wouldn't have wanted the neighbours to know what their daughter was suffering from lest they panicked. It was, after all, hard to keep a dangerous secret in Cavel.

'But you are back now,' I said. 'You will be alright soon.'

She looked at me, listlessly. Sensing her unease, I changed the topic. 'It's raining in December. Isn't that funny?'

'Do you think we can sail paper boats, Michael?' she asked.

'Now?'

She nodded. I smiled.

You know that feeling when a wish comes true, even if for a few fleeting seconds? And just when you think you could hold on to it for a lifetime, it disappears? We did make a paper boat that night with one of the carol sheets in our pew. But we couldn't set it sailing. Instead, a few minutes later, I rushed out to call Linda and her husband. The church was full again and a limp Tracey was taken to the hospital on a stretcher. The next day, on Christmas, the bell rang ceaselessly in church, overwhelming Cavel with its ominous clanging. Her mother, humbled by the incident, came home twice to enquire about what had transpired between us, probably worried that her daughter had told me of her illness. I was never forthcoming.

Months later, the D'Lima couple moved to Goa for good. With their departure, this story found its end, never to be discussed again.

Now, as my eyes drift over our compound—its dry earth waiting to be quenched by the heavy, overbearing clouds—I go and stand near my balcony, searching longingly for her. When she appears, I pull out my wooden walking stick and bearing my weight on it, head down and wait patiently below the sky.

For when it rains, I will take out our crumpled paper boat, yellowed and torn at the edges, and sail it through the narrow, muddy stream. If it stops mid-way, Tracey will laugh. Then I will do what I always did best and she will hold my hands and say, 'I hate that smile of yours.'

2

THE DANCE OF LOVE

August 1958

On her twenty-first birthday, Annette Coutinho—daughter of Karen and Alfred Sebastiano Coutinho and sister of Michael—the most sought-after belle in Cavel, was finally getting engaged to her beau of three years, Joe Crasto.

Every living person in the neighbourhood, those known to the family and even otherwise, had been invited to join the celebrations at the famed Goan Catholic Club of Pius House, not very far from Pope's Colony. Annette's parents, though, weren't convinced about their daughter's choice of husband. Reason: Joe was from Mangalore, in Mysore state, which was later renamed Karnataka. Aside from sharing a border with Portuguese-ruled Goa, as well as what the Coutinhos considered a 'lamentable' version of Konkani, the Catholics of Mangalore had nothing in common with Goans.

The Catholics of Bombay, for all practical purposes, were a team. They belonged to the same church, were blessed by the same Pope and worshipped the same Lord. What separated them was community—each one with its own history. In pockets like Cavel, community also determined where you stood in the realm of class.

Here, it was the East Indian Catholics, the sons and daughters of the city's soil, who were the self-appointed cream of the neighbourhood. Most East Indians traced their ancestry to the earliest settlers who dwelled on the islands of Bombay and neighbouring Salsette. The arrival of the Portuguese and their evangelical brigade had led to the proliferation of a new group of native converts, who settled in rural pockets like Cavel where churches were being erected. One doesn't know how and when this village was christened Cavel, but the inspiration for the name is said to have come from the local fisherfolk, the Kolis, who fished in the expansive seas not too far from here. When the British gained control of the islands of Bombay, the economy boomed and thousands of Christian immigrants from the Portuguese state of Goa started making inroads here and in other neighbourhoods, in search of jobs. Overwhelmed by this massive wave of immigrants who often shared the same surnames as them, the native Christians across the islands chose to call themselves East Indians. This new identity had little to do with geography—Bombay was on the western belt of India—and more with polity. Naming themselves after the British East India Company perhaps associated them with the Europeans.

For a very long time, the East Indians of Cavel discouraged marriages outside their community. In the church, the first few rows were always reserved for the East Indians and if a Goan dared to sit there during mass, they'd throw them ugly stares before complaining to the parish priest. Things took a turn for the better when Ursula, the daughter of the Misquittas, the richest and proudest East Indians, lost her heart to a Goan baker in the area and eloped with him. This act of defiance may have earned her a bad name, making her a recurring figure in Cavel folklore even sixty years after her death, but the walls had crumbled, and it wasn't long before Goan–East Indian marriages started becoming commonplace.

Newer walls were built when Mangalorean Catholic families, just a handful, moved into Cavel. Now it was time for the Goans to make the most of their new-found snobbery. Most Mangaloreans, as history documented, had once shared the same land as the Christian Goans. Their partition story went back centuries ago, to the time when the Catholic missionaries forced them to adopt a new god. While many Goan natives hadn't shown resistance to conversion, some were still deeply entrenched in Hindu customs. And so, when the Tribunal of Inquisition was set up by the Portuguese in Goa in 1560, its autocratic policy of discouraging the Hindu way of life and the persecution that followed thereafter, along with the high taxes that were being arbitrarily imposed, didn't win favour among several locals. Worried that they were getting a raw deal, several Christians and Hindus fled southwards, resettling in regions like Mangalore. The epidemics that plagued Goa during this time, only emboldened them.

The price they paid for that flight of freedom had been brutal, especially after Tipu Sultan gained control of South Canara in the late 1700s and issued orders to seize the estates of the Mangalorean Catholics and hold the people captive. Thousands were killed during this time. But the Goans were too preoccupied with their own lives to concern themselves with those who had 'abandoned' them. They had started absorbing foreignness into their system—dressing, eating and sounding like the Latins. The Mangaloreans, proud rebels that they were, saw this life of convenience that their cousins had chosen for themselves as far too easy. Even centuries on, this backstory forgotten, the resentment continued.

In Bombay, Mangaloreans—the Mangis—had earned themselves the distinction of being too shrewd for their own good, while the Goans—the susegaads—became infamous for their laid-back attitude. None of this was true. This pigeonholing was the machination of part love, part hate and a lot of envy.

Like many others, Karen and Alfred weren't aware of this shared, complicated history that went back over four hundred years. All they knew was that the two most prominently represented Catholic communities in Bombay—apart from the East Indians—had separated, never to come together again.

'But he's Roman Catholic, mama,' Annette had argued, when Karen had bluntly refused to consider the alliance.

'Are you nuts, Anna? Do you think there's a short supply of good-looking boys in Cavel or what?' Karen asked.

'Yes! Name one decent man in Cavel.'

'Aye, I can name a hundred, including that Benjamin boy. Why don't you fall in love with him, Anna?' her mum pleaded. 'Your Joe and his family are different from us, men.'

'But Joe loves sorpotel and chorizo, just like us,' said Annette.

'He's still Mangalorean,' Alfred echoed his wife's sentiments.

'What's the difference, papa?' Annette asked.

To this, the Coutinhos could never supply a good answer.

'Mangaloreans, I tell you, cunning people,' Karen pointed out.

Her engineer husband, whose education under the Jesuits had landed him the privilege of refined articulation, was more robust in his description. 'Darling, these Mangaloreans are quite calculating. It comes naturally to these folks. It is just better that we stay away from them.'

But Karen, who wouldn't let her husband have the last word, butted in, 'They also can't jive like Goans. Ask who is Chic Chocolate, and they don't know about Bombay's best trumpeter, men. Only want to make money all the time. Shee! Such an insult to us Catholics, I tell you. And their English! What's that word you taught me, Alfi?'

'Appalling,' he said.

'Ha, same … appall and all.'

'Mama, Joe speaks English, jives, parties and plays in a jazz band, like any other Goan boy,' Annette said. 'You both are so orthodox.'

'Shut up, Anna,' Karen said. 'Oversmart you have become. Answering us back now, huh?'

'If you don't allow me to marry Joe, I will run away like that Ursula Misquitta,' Annette threatened.

The name brought on a cold silence as Annette's parents stared at their daughter, stunned. It was a while before Karen yelled, 'What you said?'

'I will run away like Ursula,' Annette repeated. She made sure that every word that tumbled out of her mouth was louder than the other.

'Open your big mouth, and I will spank you.'

That's how the arguments mostly progressed each time the topic came up. This went on until the Coutinhos attended the annual Western music festival at the Catholic Gymkhana in Marine Lines and saw Joe Crasto perform a Jim Reeves number. He bagged the best singer award, trumping the local star Benjamin da Cunha, the guitar and banjo legend who Karen had set eyes on for her daughter.

With Joe, the young lad from Mazagaon—another quaint Christian pocket in the city—rising to overnight fame in south Bombay, nobody in the Goan community saw him as Mangalorean anymore. He had become one of their kind.

Karen and Alfred, who for long feared that their daughter would pull an Ursula on them, saw this as the perfect occasion to switch tables and start flaunting him as their future son-in-law. They were still not happy with the connection, but at least socially, it seemed more acceptable. The big day was set for November, but before people from their neighbourhood forgot who Joe Crasto—the star singer of the Catholic Gymkhana— was, they decided to get their daughter engaged to him. Annette's birthday on 5 August seemed like a good occasion.

The days preceding the celebrations were hectic. Karen and her six sisters were going to prepare the snacks for the brunch. This meant a series of heated discussions on items to be included in the final menu. When it came to food, the Rosario sisters loved one-upping each other. A dish chosen by one had to be disliked by at least four others, bringing all the planning to a standstill. The sisters found a strange bonhomie in these kitchen wars. It was only when the disinterested party of husbands, in-laws, nieces, nephews and cousins was dragged in for suggestions that a solution was found.

A final menu was drawn up, with chutney sandwiches, mutton cutlets, pork sausages, chicken fry, homemade sponge cake, boiled chickpeas, fruit punch and potato chips from Ideal Wafers at Khotachi Wadi making it to the busy list.

Around two hundred people were invited to the engagement party, including select relatives of Joe who made up more than half of the guests. Joe's immediate family was reasonably large. He was the seventh among thirteen children. His mother had died a few hours after the birth of her youngest daughter, Mary.

'Not surprised,' Karen said, when Annette told her about Joe's family. 'Who wouldn't die, men, after starting a baby factory like that, huh? This is why I warned you about that Joe boy. You want to die soon, na Anna?' she asked.

'Mama, don't forget, you come from a big family too.'

'But we were just eight,' Karen said.

'Just eight? Mama, you can't even defend yourself properly,' Annette said.

'Aye, mind that language, Anna. Don't act so smart. Show some respect to me.'

'You don't deserve any respect,' Annette scoffed.

Smack! The back of her mother's hand landed so hard on her cheek that it left both of them bruised.

During those trying days, it was Michael who played mediator. His sole task was to remind his parents that their daughter was going to be in safe hands. Joe, he told them, was negotiating a plum contract with a jazz band from Calcutta that was performing at The Taj Mahal Hotel. 'He is on his way to becoming one of Bombay's biggest singing sensations.'

As Joe's best friend, this was the least he could do. Michael and Joe had met at St Xavier's College in Dhobi Talao. They were among a tiny group of boys pursuing humanities amidst a swarm of women. Friendship was inevitable. Joe was introduced to Annette during one of his many visits to Bosco Mansion. She was his first music student. He tried teaching her to play the guitar, but she was so terrible at it that he stopped within a few weeks. By then, her violent strums had damaged all the strings on Joe's guitar. To make things worse, she had also clawed into his fretboard with her long, sharp nails, leaving several gashes.

'Your sister is the worst enemy of my music,' a miffed Joe had told his friend.

Michael had been relieved. He had known of Annette's flirtatious ways and was glad his friend had not fallen for any of it.

But love happened and accidentally—somewhere between chance meetings at Marine Drive, a place they both visited to watch the sunset. Nobody knew that Annette and Joe had started meeting more often except Michael's wife, Merlyn. On Sundays, Annette would leave with Merlyn for Chira Bazaar fish market—ostensibly to give her sister-in-law company— but would then make a detour and rush to Joe's aunt Lucy's home in Sonapur Galli. Aunty Lucy, who lived within shouting distance of Dr D'Lima Street, was privy to their romance. Here, Annette would spend the next hour or so, either watching Joe practice with his musician friends or gossiping with his aunt.

Annette would join her sister-in-law outside the fish market an hour later, and the two would go back home together. The century-old market was like any other squalid bazaar, its broken tiles, open drains and rotting stench making it hard on anyone manoeuvring its narrow gullies. But Merlyn found the market warm and welcoming. The cacophony of fisherwomen haggling with customers, convincing them of their good catch, the endless chit-chat and the continuous replenishing of baskets with fresh stock of pomfret, prawn, mackerel and Bombay duck—it reminded her of her village in Goa. Here she never felt homesick, and so she was never irritated if Annette showed up late. She didn't even grudge Annette those private moments with her boyfriend. After all, most great love stories, including her own, had begun as a dirty secret.

But Joe and Annette never enjoyed a private moment. Their only time alone was the last five minutes of that prized weekly meeting when Joe would drop Annette back to the market. He would try to sneak in a kiss, but she would reciprocate grudgingly with a peck on his cheek.

'After we get married,' she would say.

'You play so hard to get, my lovely Anna,' he'd say.

Annette would look at him disinterestedly, and then go on her usual trip about how Catholics were supposed to abstain from all pleasures until the right time. She had grown tired of telling him off repeatedly.

One day, when on an impulse Joe reached for her hand on the staircase of Aunt Lucy's home to draw her closer to his face, she dug her nails deep into his flesh and said, 'The day I am ready to kiss, you would just know.'

Her voice was cold and distant.

'Really! How?' Joe was in terrible pain, but stayed calm, refusing to let Annette have the upper hand in the argument.

'You'd just know,' she said and loosened her grip. Joe bemoaned his fate as that of any Catholic boy of his time.

When Michael eventually learnt of the affair, he wasn't very happy. It was not that he didn't trust his friend with his sister;

he just thought Joe deserved better. And his fears weren't unfounded, considering his sister's wavering conduct in the past. She always fought hard to get the things she wanted, and when they were hers, she abandoned them like they had never mattered at all. The last time Annette had brought the house down was when she applied for admission to a medical school. A reluctant Alfred Coutinho gave in and sold his property in Panjim to fund his daughter's education. But Annette had backed out within the second year, shocking everyone except Michael. The same thing happened when she learned to play the guitar, took a typing course at Davar's College in Fort and studied for a teacher's degree. Nothing had been completed. Michael had seen the development of a disturbing pattern that was incredibly hard to ignore.

Joe had been warned of his fate, but try telling a lover that love is not good for him. If you get a smile in return for your unsolicited advice, be assured that even though you were heard by the tiniest germ that swam the air at that moment, the pair of ears that the advice was meant for had cut out the disturbing sound frequencies before you had even emitted them. Love makes you dreamy, deaf and dumb—a mute, floaty, gullible victim to the cruelties of that head-spinning feeling.

When the day of the engagement arrived, Michael thought it was finally time he let go of his anxieties and fears concerning his sister, for his own sanity and that of his friend.

The hall at the Goan Catholic Club had not seen a busier afternoon in a while. Cavel had had a dry spell with not a single wedding taking place in over two years. Joe and Annette were hopefully going to break that jinx. When not used to celebrate community parties, the club functioned as a makeshift Bible reading room and an in-house sporting den for table-tennis and carrom aficionados. Today, the boards and tables had been neatly stacked in one corner of the hall, and the bookshelves had been covered with white cloth.

The guests occupied every inch of space in the hall. But here's the thing about people from different communities coming together—the results are never flattering. Just as the Coutinhos had predicted, the crowd had marked their territories with the Goans and East Indians choosing to occupy the right side of the hall and the Mangaloreans making themselves comfortable at the other end.

It wasn't impossible to identify one from the other. The Goan and East Indian women came in their Sunday best, flaunting floral dresses and skirts that matched their printed blouses, with their hair pinned up in a bob-shaped bouffant— the work of Cavel's most popular hairstylist, Sylvia Menezes, who had not eaten a morsel since morning because of her back-to-back appointments. The Mangalorean women, on the other hand, were decked out in heavy embroidered sarees. Some of the older aunties even had tiny jasmine garlands knotted in their hair buns. The men looked just like each other, more or less: plain white cotton shirts with black trousers. Karen, however, identified the quieter ones, those with a permanent deadpan expression on their face, as members of Joe's family.

'Aye, they look like they've come for a funeral, men,' she told Alfred.

'Shush,' her husband said, hoping that nobody had overheard her. 'This is not the right time or place to grieve about not getting a Goan son-in-law.'

'I am just telling you a fact, Alfi,' she said. 'My poor daughter. So innocent she is, men. She doesn't know what these Mangaloreans are.'

'Our daughter isn't innocent. She knows how to find herself a groom; I am sure she will manage better than you think,' he said.

'What sad people, men,' Karen went on.

'We cannot help this anymore,' he whispered.

'But you can't stop me from talking....'

'Not here, please,' he said curtly and shut her up.

Today, Annette was the cynosure of all eyes. The young woman understood fashion like the French their wine. Whether Indian or western wear, her style, inspired by movies and magazines, was always sharp and never lazy. For the engagement function, Joe had insisted she wore a saree given by his family. Annette had agreed, but only if she were allowed to select one herself. She ended up buying a cream tussar silk with a plain red border from Dadar market. It had been too minimalistic in choice and taste for the Crasto family. But Annette, who wore the sari over a puffed sleeve blouse, like the Hindi film actresses of her time, complemented it with a gorgeous pair of gold earrings and a choker. Her customised pair of closed heels had been styled from pure leather by the famed Chinese shoemaker Charlie Bhang, of S Bhang & Company in Colaba.

The Bhangs had moved to Bombay from Calcutta twenty years earlier, venturing into the restaurant business with a Chinese eatery. But the lack of patrons for their cuisine led Charlie's father Peng to switch businesses. The shoemaking skills that Peng had acquired while working for a tannery in Calcutta salvaged the Bhangs' sinking fortunes, and they opened a shoe store and workshop not very far from the Taj Hotel. Pan SuLeh, christened Charlie, hopped into the trade in the 1940s as a twelve-year-old, drawing customers from far and wide and turning around the family's fortunes for good. In Charlie, Annette had found a great accomplice who enjoyed her taste in design and style. It was because of his shoes that she could carry her saree with such regal confidence.

When the couple entered the hall, the guests gave their metal chairs a breather. Joe's band performed an electrifying medley, which left the birthday girl beaming from ear to ear.

Sashaying like a queen, she walked past her guests towards the two-tier cake that adorned the centre of the hall. She had left her hair loose and had generously coloured her thin lips in a dark shade of maroon, making them looker fuller than usual. Twenty-one suited her. No man there could take his eyes off her. Joe, the superstar, had suddenly become secondary for the celebration.

When they reached the table, Joe handed his girlfriend the knife and affectionately held her by her slender waist—much to the disapproval of all his relatives.

The band immediately broke into the 'Happy Birthday' song, joined by the crowd. Even before they had finished singing, Annette, who was basking in all the attention, cut the cake with the precision of a surgeon, drawing a thunderous applause from the guests. This was possibly the closest she had ever come to putting her brief surgical practice at medical school to use.

After the cake-cutting, Alfred Coutinho announced the November wedding, which was followed by Fr Mathais Dias blessing the couple. Though rings were exchanged, the official wedding banns were to be announced a couple of months later. While the Crastos weren't too keen on having an engagement, the Coutinhos had pressed for it, assuring them that they'd not take a paisa from the boy's side for the ceremony. It was well known that the Coutinhos loved to celebrate in style.

The afternoon party got wilder as the men hit the floor with their partners. Alcohol wasn't served as the threat of Prohibition lingered despite having been revoked a few years ago. Both Karen and Alfred were particular about not paying the cops for anything. That didn't stop the young boys from sneaking in country whisky in Duke cola bottles. They distributed it among the men who had paid in advance for the alcohol from Tresa aunty's drinking joint in the nearby lane, a popular haunt for the wasted.

Twenty-five-year-old Benjamin da Cunha, the boy who Karen had wanted for her daughter and who was known to play the banjo with carefree abandon, drank a little too much at the engagement. He was beside himself, and everyone could see that. Because when Joe's band played the Elvis Presley number *Blue Suede Shoes*, Benjamin took to the floor as if he owned it—first flapping his arms like a bird, then wriggling the palms of his hands and his body as if a powerful stream of current were coursing through his veins. You couldn't ignore him, as his head rapidly drew shapes in the air as the lyrics of the song played out for him. The crowd actually thought that Benjamin had had a stroke as he pitched his head up towards the right side when the band singer sang, 'Well, you can knock me down,' and then swung it down when the singer followed up with 'Step in my face;' he continued by moving his head towards the left to repeat the same motions as the song went on, 'Slander my name, all over the place.'

If that wasn't dizzying enough, Benjamin broke into a rather vulgar swing which resembled a series of pelvic thrusts, even as the lines continued on a loop. 'Blue, blue, blue suede shoes. Blue, blue, blue suede shoes, yeah! Blue, blue, blue, suede shoes, baby.' Here, he improvised a little, keying in a twist, bending his knees down slowly while twirling his waist, before lifting himself to show off his power-packed thrusts once again. His entire body seemed to have been possessed by some irrepressible energy which was both amusing and off-putting at the same time.

Repulsed by the performance, the crowd scattered and allowed Benjamin to take complete control of the dance floor. The Mangalorean aunties who until then had only been gossiping about poor Joe's fate now silently prayed harder to keep drunk, silly Goan men away from their daughters.

But Benjamin's obnoxious dexterity on the dance floor hadn't been triggered by the peppy Presley number or the alcohol. In fact, there was a long history of crushed hopes and desires that had led to this manic fit. Benjamin, who was popularly known as Banjo Man in Cavel, had been in love with the girl who was now engaged to Joe. And while Annette hadn't done a thing to set his heart aflutter, her mother Karen was partly responsible for his condition, having sown tiny seeds of love in Benjamin's heart ever since he could remember. Each time she met him, she'd address him as her future zhaavei. The sound of it had worked like magic. He had started swimming in the idea of being Annette's husband.

Benjamin had secretly harboured dreams of winning Annette's heart since he was eighteen. On several occasions, he had deliberately bumped into Annette in the compound so that he could strike up a conversation with her. That he was incredibly nervous and failed to prolong it beyond the niceties of 'hi' and 'hello' was a shame. But he was confident that he would someday be hers, and she his—all thanks to the blessings he had already secured from his future mother-in-law. He was surprised how one dramatic loss at the Catholic Gymkhana music fest had changed his fortunes. If only Karen had told him that his fate was clinging to that win, he would have braved all odds to snatch the trophy from Joe. Alas, things were not meant to be the way he had planned. And now here he was, fighting his grief on the dance floor, drunk beyond redemption, making a spectacle of himself in front of his friends and family.

Joe cornered an amused Michael, asking if anything could be done to get the lad off the dance floor.

'He has lost his marbles, hasn't he?' Joe enquired. 'My family will walk off any moment. You know how they are. They already warned me about those drunk, susegaad Goans and now Benjamin is giving them proof.'

'Let the song end, we will take him aside,' Michael suggested.

Meanwhile, Karen hung her head in shame, embarrassed that she had once even considered Benjamin for Annette. 'This is what you wanted our daughter to marry?' Alfred asked as he saw Benjamin wiggle.

'He is drunk, men, Alfi,' Karen said innocently.

'That's not the point. Did you know he danced like that?'

Among the mortified people in the hall, one person watched Benjamin intently. Her gaze remained fixed in his direction, observing how he moved his body in perfect rhythm to the song. It was Annette's favourite rock 'n' roll number, and she hadn't seen anyone encapsulate the energy of this particular song the way she imagined Elvis would have.

Watching Benjamin was like seeing Elvis on the floor. Annette revelled in her unexpected fan girl moment and drank it up one dance move at a time. She didn't realise when this excitement transformed into something entirely different. How it all happened within a matter of seconds, one cannot say.

But as Annette kept ogling Benjamin, a nervous chill ran down her spine, filling her insides with a tingling sensation—something she had never experienced before. She could feel her body unravel as Benjamin's every twist released an inexplicable spark inside her.

She continued sizing him up, her eyes frozen in his direction as if everything else around had never existed. It was only when the music stopped, and Benjamin's friends quickly moved him to the side of the room that she snapped out of her trance.

By then, Annette was gasping for breath. To regain composure, she asked Julian, her sixteen-year-old cousin, if he would oblige her with a sip of his cola. 'My throat feels dry.'

Julian didn't dare mention that he was drinking whisky for fear that his cousin would tell on him. Assuming that she wouldn't know the difference, he gave her the bottle anyway. She downed the entire drink in a gulp. 'What did you do, you fool? You finished my cola,' Julian snapped.

Annette stared at him blankly, her eyes going hazy, her legs faltering and her head twirling in loops. Julian snatched the bottle from her and sped away as she found a place to sit.

She plonked on the chair and gently massaged her head with her fingers, trying to battle the confusion plaguing her brain. Not able to make any sense of the trick that her mind was playing, she continued to rub her forehead, curling and uncurling her fingers as she moved them on the taut skin of her face.

The guests were so busy in their own merriment that they didn't notice how hearts were slowly breaking away from each other, galvanising some to change their course of action. Was it the music, was it the dance or was it the drink? Was it everything, and love? A tumultuous flood of incomprehensible emotions zoomed through Annette, refusing to vanish. She could recall nothing now, apart from the body she was aching for.

Sitting across from Annette was Benjamin, slumped against the metal chair. The humiliation he had brought upon himself was discernible as he sat heavily with his head hanging down in shame. He was probably wondering how he had got himself here and how he could rescue himself from the situation. Annette searched for his face, now buried in the palms of his hands.

A few minutes later, she got up from her seat and sashaying like a queen—albeit a tipsy one—gift-wrapped in tussar silk, she walked past the guests, swung towards Benjamin, and pulled him up by the hand to lead him outside the hall.

Nobody knew why the young lady had suddenly disappeared from the party. Nobody, except Joe Crasto, the boy from Mazagaon and the star singer of the Catholic Gymkhana, who had just lost his love and promised kiss to *Blue Suede Shoes*.

3

THE EXORCISM OF
MICHAEL COUTINHO

March 1997

Merlyn Coutinho's life turned on its head the day she found several half-eaten chikus strewn around her backyard. From then on, fallen fruits had become a common sight in her garden.

Once every week, on a Monday, the maali came to help her trim the shrubs that she reared behind her ground-floor home at Bosco Mansion. He'd pile them up in his lopsided garden cart and dump them at the nearby municipal garbage dump for an extra twenty rupees. The state of her fruits broke Merlyn's heart.

Only a fortunate few in Pope's Colony had a backyard to call their own and Merlyn made sure she used hers to the hilt, converting it into an ornamental green lung where rose mallows, petunias and periwinkles grew alongside potted tomatoes, brinjals and chillies. Her most prized plant, however, was the waywardly growing gigantic chiku tree, an heirloom which had now become a sore point between Merlyn and her husband Michael, who she suspected had a role to play in the gruesome murder of her fruits.

'You ate my chikus, na? Tell me ... tell me, re. Give me an answer,' Merlyn would say.

'Foolish lady, you have gone mad,' was how her scowling husband responded, mostly.

Merlyn's suspicions had first taken root when she caught her husband red-handed, plucking fruits from the tree. In his defence, Michael had only interfered in his wife's gardening chores because a particular bunch of over-ripe chikus had overwhelmed the house with its unpleasant, fermenting scent. He had always been allergic to rotting smells and hated this one the most. The only reason he chose to keep this from his wife was that he found it too silly an issue to bother her with.

So when the irritation in his nostrils got extremely severe, he decided it was time to nip it in the bud. Sometime after the couple had eaten lunch and Merlyn had gone to her room to take a nap, he went to the backyard to trace the source of the rot. Little did he know that his wife, who was hell-bent on getting hold of the culprit behind the killing of her fruits, had followed him out and was surreptitiously watching him from the kitchen that overlooked the backyard.

After going around in circles for several minutes, Michael had found the problematic cluster. Hanging loosely from a branch that bent towards the kitchen window, this squashed bunch of chikus had been infested by a horde of flies.

He got hold of a creaky wooden ladder and carefully climbed up one step at a time. When he was close enough, he knifed the bunch and let the fruits drop. He had wanted to throw the chikus away, but Merlyn had rushed out by then. She had found a culprit for the fruits that were disappearing from her tree and falling to the ground.

'I knew it. I knew it ... haav zannam,' she yelled as Michael clambered down the ladder.

'Knew what?' he asked, surprised.

'That you are killing my chikus,' she said.

'No, I didn't,' he said brusquely.

Though he had flatly denied any involvement, from that day on his wife had turned into an annoying nag—reminding him every day of how he had ruined her backyard by first wantonly biting into her 'precious' chikus and then throwing them back into the garden. One night, she tried picking a fight with him while he was struggling to sleep. That was when Michael lost his cool. He refused to play to his wife's whims and fancies, packed his clothes into his black VIP suitcase and immediately left for his parents' home. The house was on the floor right above theirs, so logistically at least, it seemed like a very sound move for that hour of the night.

—-—

It had been fourteen weeks since he moved out. Since his parents had long passed away, Michael now lived with his widowed sister Annette in their family home. The two had never got along, even as kids, and Michael's return had made things worse. Their squabbles could be heard all through the day. Every resident in 193-A, Bosco Mansion was privy to their fights—thanks to the building's wooden exterior, which did not allow for any sound-proofing.

But the full-blown arguments with his sister aside, Michael didn't consider going back to his wife of forty-five years anytime soon. He was tired, not with her as much as with the idea of living with her. Over the last ten years or so, especially after their kids had moved to Canada, Merlyn's universe had shrunk considerably. Her life now revolved only around her garden, husband and home. She had no friends, except for her neighbour Ellena and his sister Annette, both of whom he detested. This insular life that she found comfort in had made her so myopic that she could no longer see things for what they were.

His children, Ryan and Sarah, were aghast that their parents had even considered separation at this age, and that too, over a chiku tree.

'Please don't embarrass us,' Ryan told his dad over the phone.

'Take your mum to Canada, live with her for forty-five years and then do all this patronising talk,' Michael said, irritated.

Merlyn too had made zero attempts to mend the broken ties, more because even after he had left home, the half-eaten chikus hadn't stopped popping down from her tree.

She vented to Laxmi, her maid, in broken Hindi saying, '*Hamara aadmi still nikalos chikus upar se. You know, he eats them thoda and throws them neeche. Mere ko bahut trouble karta.*'

Merlyn had invented this ingenious mish mash of Hindi and English—two languages she was not comfortable speaking—to converse with her maid. Though mostly incomprehensible, it helped communicate the little details that mattered and got the job done. '*Khana cook karne ko hain.*' '*Do the jhadoo.*' '*Hamara tea banao.*' '*Kapda saabun main dip karo please.*' '*Water bageecha main pheko.*' The list was endless.

Sometimes Merlyn stretched her absurd language experiments slightly, using fuller, longer sentences. But Laxmi had smartened up. Today, for instance, she was able to conclude that Michael saab had been up to some mischief. She pacified her memsaab by suggesting, once again, that her husband be taken to a tantrik who would exorcise him.

In an ideal situation, Merlyn would never have considered a witch doctor. But Michael's twisted and unforgivable chiku-eating habits had left many a knot in her mind. Why did he steal the fruits when he could simply ask Merlyn to pluck them for him? Why did he only gnaw at half the fruit? Why did he throw the half-eaten chikus in the backyard when there was a garbage bin at home?

All these questions tormented Merlyn night and day. These were the same questions that Michael saw as glaring evidence to absolve him of the crime. But his wife had been blinded by a bizarre theory.

For some reason, Merlyn believed that her husband was haunted by the ghost of his mother, Karen, who had died twenty years ago. She had loved biting into the soft and pulpy flesh of the chiku fruit.

Merlyn recalled how in the early years of her marriage, when they lived on the upper floor with the rest of the family, Karen would hand-pick the ripe fruits from a huge branch that could be accessed from her balcony and eat them all alone. Sometimes, if she got a few extra, she'd make a chiku milkshake which she grudgingly shared with the rest of the family.

At the time, the house Merlyn and Michael currently lived in was unoccupied. But the chiku tree that had been left by the previous owners—the D'Lima family—flourished under

Karen's care. The tree, which was a few inches taller than Bosco Mansion and wide enough to cover half the building, was watered each day through a hosepipe that ran from Karen's house down to the lawn.

Years later, even after Karen had taken ill due to dementia, she continued plucking and eating the fruits. By then Michael and Merlyn had bought the flat on the ground-floor and were the proud owners of a house with a backyard. While the old lady was happy for her son, it affected her a great deal to imagine that her daughter-in-law now owned the tree which she had nurtured for so long.

Embittered, she found weird ways to harass Merlyn. Every once in a while, a half-eaten chiku would drop into the backyard from the first floor. When her daughter-in-law questioned her, Karen would feign innocence.

'It has to be sasumai's kaam,' Merlyn told Laxmi.

The thought seemed bizarre, but the circumstances did not allow her to think differently. Also, her capricious husband and silly maid weren't helping. In fact, by giving in to her fantastical logic—one by refusing to explain himself, and the other by suggesting exorcism—they only ensured that the crazy thoughts thrived and prevailed. To add to that, Merlyn's children, the only souls with the capacity to reason, didn't live close by. There was practically nobody to drive sense into the mind of the sixty-three-year-old woman.

Michael used the brief estrangement to ponder upon his life—how it was now and how it had been. He had married Merlyn very young. At twenty-two, when he was still struggling to make it as a firebrand journalist, he had met his future wife at the Church of the Holy Name in Colaba, which over a decade later would be elevated to the status of a cathedral. This was the first time he had entered a church in eight years—the last being the midnight mass of Christmas Eve, 1945. He had made this exception for an exclusive interview with the Archbishop of Bombay on the seething issue of the harassment of the Christian minority in the city. It turned out that the Cardinal was not in his office, but in church, overseeing preparations for a huge celebratory mass. His staff was with him, and that was how Michael happened to meet Merlyn Ermelinda Mascarenhas, an eighteen-year-old from Calapor, Goa, who had completed her final school exam in Portuguese and had only recently secured a job as a typist at a shipping company in Bombay. She had come with her father Pedro, who worked at the Archdiocese's office, to take the Cardinal's blessings for her new journey.

Four years before this, Pedro, a widower, had married an East Indian woman from Khotachi Wadi, an East Indian village in Girgaum which was just a kilometre away from Cavel, and had moved into her gorgeous bungalow. He had lost his first wife when Merlyn was only five years old. Hoping to secure a good life for his child, he had left her in the care of his mother and come to Bombay where he found the job of a clerk at the Archdiocese's office. He had befriended his future wife, Coleen Ferreira, a music conductor and choir singer, at St Francis Xavier's Church in Dabul where he attended mass every Sunday. The truth was that he only went for mass to listen to her sing those Latin hymns in her operatic voice. Several years into these musical indulgences, he had finally found the courage to tell Coleen how much he liked listening to her. Soon he had joined the choir himself and spent most of his free time at Coleen's house, where she lived with her mother. She had lost her father and two brothers in a ship blast nearly a decade ago, and her four sisters had long married and settled comfortably into the routines of family life.

Seeing their friendship blossom, Coleen's mother suggested Pedro marry her daughter, who was forty and by this time had lost any hope of finding herself a groom. Pedro had been lonely too, and his fondness for Coleen wasn't a secret. They had married in a private ceremony in the presence of a priest, Coleen's mother and a few other relatives, including Merlyn, who was just fourteen years old and was visiting Bombay for the first time.

While Pedro had thought it would be a nice idea to let Merlyn stay in Goa, Coleen had insisted that he bring her back so that they could live as a family. Pedro waited another three years for Merlyn to complete her schooling before bringing her back to Bombay. Under Coleen's guidance, Merlyn had learnt to rustle up two square meals a day. She was also learning to play the piano and had been initiated into English when, eight months later, Coleen, who felt that her step-daughter had turned into a confident young woman, found her a job so she could experience life outside her home.

Michael vividly remembered the moment he set eyes on Merlyn Ermelinda. She had been sitting quietly in church, waiting for her turn to meet the head priest. The gold and bronze hue of the intricately painted frescoes which decorated the ceilings of the church, and the bright colours of the stained-glass artwork on the altar, magnified by the filtering light of the sun, appeared to have captivated the girl. He had snapped her out of her reverie when he introduced himself. At least for her, it was love at first sight.

Their courtship spanned about five months. Michael would sneak a meeting during her lunch break, spending time with her over keema pav and raspberry soda at the Irani cafe, Yazdani, in Fort, before heading to his office near the fishing port of Sassoon Docks in Colaba. What Michael found most appealing about Merlyn was that she wasn't pretentious. She struggled with English and made no bones about it as she conversed with him in Konkani. Unfortunately, he barely understood the language thanks to his parents, who believed that living in Cavel meant following in the light of the East Indians and Goans of their town—the Anglicised lot. Whenever they met, which was thrice a week, they'd exchange notes. He bought her books so she could pick up the English she needed to get by at work, and he'd plead with her to teach him how to say 'I love you' in Konkani.

Their romantic rendezvous suffered a small setback when Merlyn's father found out about their dates. He told Michael straight off: 'Either you make her your bride now or forget her for good.'

Michael and Merlyn had tied the knot in November 1953, six months after they first met. Merlyn continued working but quit her job two years later when their daughter Sarah was born. Marriage, however, had not been a walk in the park. The couple experienced the initial strain in their relationship when they observed their first season of Lent together. Michael was to learn that his demure Konkani-speaking wife—staunch and conservative Goan Catholic that she was—survived only on pez (the humble rice gruel), during the forty days of fasting observed by Christians to remember Christ's journey into the arid desert and the sacrifices he made before he was crucified. Worse, she had plans to impose the practice on every member of the family and even threatened to leave home if the custom was not taken seriously.

Mama Karen had never been pleased with this union. After her dreams of marrying her son to the D'Lima heiress had come to nought, she had shortlisted other lucrative prospects from Cavel and the neighbouring lane, Dabul. One could only imagine her disappointment when Michael found himself a bride who couldn't even string together a sentence in English. That she was related, even if not directly, to the elite Ferreiras of Khotachi Wadi had helped Karen keep face.

Nothing, however, had caused Karen more stress than when her daughter-in-law threatened to bring the house down with her ludicrous demand that pez be cooked daily.

Fearing that Merlyn would abandon the home over the issue and bring much shame to the family, Karen convinced all the meat-eating members to pay heed. Michael, a self-proclaimed agnostic, was perturbed by his wife's determination to convert the Coutinho family that loved their sorpotel and mutton xacuti even during Lent into hardcore rice and pickle eaters.

The tradition had continued to date, but with every passing season of Lent, Michael observed how his love for his wife was losing its sheen. For a long time, he blamed it on Lent. When his relationship with Merlyn was beyond help, ten years into their marriage, his now-dead friend Joe had claimed that abandoning copulation for forty days every year had played a significant role in the slow decay of their love.

'This is a big sin. No shame only you have re,' Merlyn would tell Michael and make the sign of the cross when he drew closer to her in bed. The couple didn't realise when the forty-day abstinence from sex extended to indefinite physical asceticism. Once that happened, neither party made the first move, shamed mostly by age—a sagacious reminder of the carnal tidings of their youth.

Looking back, Michael could tell where he and his wife had failed as a couple, and why Merlyn had turned into the empty-headed monster that she now was. She acted without much thought and often too quickly. It would pass, he assured himself. Until then, Michael Coutinho would have to survive under the same roof as his sister, the one person he blamed for the untimely death of his only best friend, Joe.

'It has to be the ghost of sasumai,' Merlyn thought to herself again. But she knew her parish priest, Fr Eugene D'Souza, wouldn't buy this. She also feared speaking about exorcism to him because she had learnt from a fellow parishioner that a priest from a nearby church who prayed over the so-called possessed had recently been packed off to a village in Thane. It was a controversial subject, and no priest would entertain her. That was why she conceded to Laxmi's suggestion to have the tantrik come over. The issue at hand, however, was convincing Michael to be exorcised.

Would the old man believe that he was possessed by the ghost of his mother? 'I don't think so,' Annette told Merlyn over the phone. She even wondered aloud if her mama loved chikus so much that she'd haunt her son twenty years after her death.

But Annette would give her hands and legs to have Michael out of her house. This was why she agreed to her sister-in-law's ridiculous plan.

'Come to think of it, mama did love chikus,' she informed Merlyn the next time she called. 'These days I see her in my dreams too. What if mama wants to take baba with her?'

Her sister-in-law's suspicion drove Merlyn to the edge. No way would she allow that to happen. Her mother-in-law had troubled her enough in the last few years before she died. If she had plans to take Michael, Merlyn was ready to put up a fight.

'I want my Mike back,' she said between sobs.

'Yes, yes, we have to do something,' Annette repeated, feigning concern.

When her fears got too unbearable, Merlyn punctured her ego and went to meet her husband at his house one Sunday afternoon. Annette opened the door for Merlyn, who was carrying a stainless steel dabba in one hand and four laadis of brun pao, wrapped in an old newspaper, in the other.

As soon as she walked in, Merlyn started searching for Michael.

'Where's Michael re?' she asked.

'He is in the bedroom, watching a movie.'

'He ate food?'

'You're just in time,' Annette assured her.

'You think he will eat my khana?' Merlyn asked her sister-in-law.

'I am sure. Your plan is good,' Annette winked.

Merlyn headed to the dining table and laid out the food and chinaware. When she was done, she went to placate her husband.

The Coutinho home, like the other flats in Bosco Mansion, was an architectural marvel. It had a warren of rooms, each with two large doors—one that led to the bathroom or balcony and another to the drawing room or a bedroom. It was a maze that took some time to get accustomed to. Space was never wanting here, and the sprawling arched windows, two for every room, ensured that the house was bathed in light during the day. The furniture was vintage, dating back to when the father of Alfred Coutinho, Sebastiano Marcus, had moved into this newly built structure in 1913 with his wife Maria and their four children after arriving on a steamboat from Goa. He had rented the space from the Catholic Fellowship Trust, giving a substantial down payment for the tenancy rights. It had been their home from that day on. The arched wooden three-seater sofa set, the mahogany bookshelf and the teak cupboards had withstood the wear and tear of time. Annette had added nothing new to the flat, except for littering it with her magazines and books. She had been shoddy with its upkeep.

When Michael had come here three months ago, he had moved into his old bedroom, the one that he and his wife had lived in for nearly a decade. The room had an old television set which was also Michael's. He had left it here after his daughter, Sarah, had bought her parents a new one from Vijay Sales during a visit last year.

The Hindi film *Sholay* was playing on television today—not that Michael was watching. He was fast asleep, snoring loudly, as the song *Mehbooba* blared in the room. Watching Helen gyrate to the song, Merlyn remembered the days of her youth when she too had a curvy waist like the one the actress was rhythmically swaying on television. She remembered how Michael had once lovingly called her 'my Helen'. Today, her nicknames oscillated between devil, fool, monster, and sometimes just Merlyn. None of them reminded her of the actress.

She went closer to him and tried waking him up as she had aeons ago, gently stroking the loose folds of skin on his forehead. It had been so long since she last touched him so affectionately. She noticed how quickly he had aged in the last few weeks of being away from her. The movement of her light fingers on his head was enough to stir him from his slumber.

'What are you doing here?' he snapped.

'*Jevon haadla* ... it's on the table,' she said partly in Konkani. 'Come eat,' she added.

'I don't want your pez.' Michael rebuffed her immediately.

'I made sorpotel.' And without waiting for a reaction from him, Merlyn walked out of the room quietly.

Michael's mouth was wide open. He could barely believe what he had just heard. Sorpotel during Lent! Was this the miracle of a brief separation, he wondered.

The trio sat through the meal quietly. *Sholay's* villain, Gabbar, whose voice boomed from the other room, made up for the silence with his heavy-handed dialogues. It was Annette who finally spoke. 'Michael, you should go back home. See what Merlyn did today. Isn't this enough proof of how much she loves you?'

'Then tell the woman to stop accusing me of things I haven't done,' Michael said, without looking at Merlyn. His voice bore the obduracy of a child.

'So you didn't eat the chikus?' Annette asked.

'Don't be silly.'

Merlyn was angry but decided not to show it. She slowly lifted her ageing body from the chair and went to pick up her husband's plate which he had wiped clean, licking up the vinegary gravy and crumbs of pao. She could feel her stomach churn and twist, having broken her fast which she had held on to steadfastly ever since she had been a child, making an exception only during one of her pregnancies when she suffered from an iron deficiency. In return for the transgression, she would light a candle at each and every church in Mumbai, she promised God.

'Okay, I am sorry re,' said Merlyn. '*Ghara yo* … please.'

Six hours later, Michael was in his own bed with Merlyn lying beside him. Another Lenten vow had been broken. The old woman was blushing with embarrassment even as her fingers toyed with her husband's scanty chest hair. They were both exhausted by the ravages of love. Their last time seemed so long ago in history that this now felt like a first, but in another time and place.

'I missed you,' he told her.

Merlyn smiled, but at the back of her mind she was panicking. Had she just made love to the soul of her sasumai?

The next couple of days, however, were so dreamy that Merlyn did not dare mention her plans of calling the tantrik. She only panicked again when she found a few half-eaten chikus in their bedroom.

'The saitaan has become powerful. Something has to be done re,' she told Annette and her maid.

At Laxmi's behest, the tantrik agreed to show up on Saturday afternoon. Merlyn checked her calendar; they just had a day to break it to Michael. At the last minute, Annette came up with a solution. 'Drop a few sleeping tablets into his tea in the morning. He will sleep through all of this.'

That was the plan. And it seemed to be working well. Michael had fallen asleep on their sofa while reading his newspaper. The tantrik, who wore his long dreadlocks down, sat on the floor with his witchcraft wares evenly spread out in a circle around the furniture.

The baba had come in a long black robe, just like in the B-grade movies, and was covered with mystical chains that had tiny skull heads for pendants. The only thing Merlyn recognised was the string of prayer beads in his hand which she had seen a Hindu pujari carry. His eccentric attire had kept Merlyn distracted through the ritual. But an hour later—after the tantrik had finished chanting his prayers and the effect of the pills was expected to wane—when Michael did not wake up, Merlyn began to worry. They splashed cold water on his face, but Michael still would not move. She checked his pulse, and it was slowing steadily.

Call it divine intervention or Mother Nature's biggest joke on the Coutinhos: the very next moment, a storm broke. Strong winds began blowing, and the branches of the chiku tree in the backyard swayed from corner to corner.

The tantrik had found another purpose. 'Your mother-in-law is taking him,' he said. Suddenly he began moving his eyeballs rapidly in odd directions and hollered, 'I can see her … I can see her.'

All hell broke loose in the Coutinho home. Merlyn began wailing in despair; Annette, who had come to witness the exorcism, started panicking too.

'Should we call the doctor?' Annette asked.

'No. Cut down the tree. Cut it right now,' the tantrik ordered. 'The bhoot is attached to the tree, not to your brother. It's your last chance to save him.'

Merlyn was determined not to let her mother-in-law take her husband away. In her head, she had already declared war on the ghost.

Her knees had been giving her a hard time of late. Despite how much it hurt, she limped to the backyard—now a quagmire because of the shower that had accompanied the storm—and dug out her garden tools. She brought out a hatchet and two chisels and asked her sister-in-law and maid to give her a hand, as they started chopping the tree down. Merlyn's energy belied her age as she thumped her hatchet with great fury right into the heart of the trunk.

Heavy winds continued to blow. For the next ten minutes, the trio kept their delicate, frail arms occupied in the futile task. Despite their grave efforts, they had only managed to make small dents. Nonetheless, the repeated stabbing, along with the wind, was good enough to rattle the branches of the chiku tree.

That was when Laxmi saw a big, dangerous creature with chikus in its mouth jump down from the tree. It was large enough for the other two women to take notice. They froze in their places, and their faces quickly changed colour—from utter shock and dismay to collective mortification. Merlyn sucked in a mouthful of air, gulping her folly down one deep breath at a time.

Right then, they heard Michael's screams from within the house. He had regained consciousness and was cussing the tantrik out, baffled as to why a man who looked like he was at a fancy-dress party was swirling around him and not allowing him to escape.

'Who the hell is he?' he asked his wife, when she rushed in. She stood helplessly, not knowing what to say.

But outside, the injured tree made a sudden, unanticipated fall. Knocked down by a strong gust of wind, the tree broke through their kitchen window and damaged the side of their house. The thud quieted all of them. The silence was broken moments later when the tantrik announced, 'His mother's spirit has left him. Your husband has been rescued from the snares of death.'

It took Michael a moment to make sense of the entire spectacle.

Horrified, he made a lunge for the tantrik and holding him by his hair, began to throw weak punches at his face.

'*Maar naka*,' Merlyn pleaded.

Michael looked pointedly at his wife, his voice seething with rage. 'Merlyn, you idiot, you fool. How could you not figure out that this was the work of a damn rat?'

4

A PENCIL DISAPPEARED

April 1944

The morning of 14 April had been a surreal one for Mario Lawrence. His father David had come into the room twice, tapping him gently on his shoulder, then pulling down his chador and even sprinkling water on his face to whisk him off the straw mat on which he had been sleeping. None of it had worked. He continued to feign sleep.

Waking up Mario for school was always a ceremony in itself. Sometimes, when repeatedly calling his name elicited no response, David would carry the boy on his shoulder and take him to the bathroom. His wife Tresa would then get Mario to sit on the stool, balancing him on it with the help of her husband before splashing mugs of warm water on their son's head. Only then would the boy open his eyes, which he had deliberately shut tight. Mario hated school. He did not like being around other children, detested talking to them, and most importantly, loathed studying.

But 14 April had been different. Years later, while narrating to his wife how events had unfolded on that particular day,

Michael Coutinho would describe it as the 'happiest morning of Mario's life.'

That day too, Mario had pretended to be fast asleep. But the charade ended when his father bent down and whispered, 'Wake up, baba. See your gift.'

The mention of a gift stirred him. As soon as his father had left the room, Mario opened his eyes and combed through his bedding, searching under the sheet and the mat when a red cardboard box caught his attention. The box was sitting on the edge of his pillow with a note attached to it: 'Happy Birthday, baba!'

He grabbed the box, moved his fingers and nimbly opened it. Twelve sharpened graphite points stared back at him. When he pulled them out all at once, he could no longer contain his excitement. Nobody in his class had ever owned pencils with eraser tips.

He ran out of the room to his parents, who were in the kitchen and broke into a happy jig while flaunting his new pencils. David and Tresa were overwhelmed; they couldn't remember the last time their seven-year-old son looked so happy.

Mario wasn't a problem child, but he lacked the predictability and enthusiasm of kids his age. He was timid by nature and rarely spoke, except to his parents and their thirteen-year-old neighbour, Michael. That too needed some effort and prodding, as Mario's answers were often monosyllabic. He preferred being a recluse, living in his bubble.

His parents were protective of him, and but naturally. Mario's birth had been nothing short of a miracle. Tresa had suffered four miscarriages and had given up all hope of having a child when Mario was conceived ten years into her marriage. Those nine months after conception had been excruciating— the fear of another miscarriage looming every day. When he was finally born, and Tresa had become a mother, everything else had felt like a bad dream.

But the years following Mario's birth hadn't been as reassuring, because his oddities began to surface slowly. For starters, he didn't like being around people; it made him nervous and edgy and sometimes even aggressive. In Cavel, people found his behaviour nothing short of obnoxious.

Dr Ralph McGowan, the Anglo-Indian physician who ran a clinic in Chira Bazaar, described him as an over-sensitive and anti-social child. While he hadn't been able to diagnose Mario's condition from his readings on the behavioural sciences, Dr McGowan was able to conclude that Mario was susceptible to emotional instability. His parents had been warned against admonishing him or indulging in any form of corporal punishment.

'Shield his nerves,' the doctor had advised.

But Mario's self-inflicted isolation had not come without advantages. The boy was extraordinarily gifted. If he wasn't studying or playing with kids his age, it was also because he had found himself a healthy preoccupation. He spent hours sketching the faces of people on paper. Some of these portraits were too good to be true. To encourage his son's passion, David had requested his friend Pedro, a tarvotti (sailor) on a steamer that sailed between Great Britain and Calcutta, to get his son a set of drawing pencils from London. He had heard that they made pencils only for sketching. The timing had been just right, with Pedro bringing the gift a few weeks before

Mario's birthday. The box of drawing pencils had cost David, who made a modest salary as a fireman with the Bombay Fire Brigade, a fortune. But he knew how happy it would make his son, and that was all that mattered.

'Pai, I take pencils to school?' Mario asked his father in broken English. The fact that Mario had even cared to string a sentence together proved that the pencils meant a great deal to him.

'Yes, but only take one,' David told his son. 'You see, baba, these pencils are very dear, so use it carefully. Don't sharpen it. I will do it for you. Okay?'

'Thank you, pai.'

An hour later, Mario was in front of Michael's house, knocking incessantly till Perpetual, the Coutinhos', housemaid answered the door.

'*Kaun ha tinga?*' Perpetual asked in Konkani.

Mario didn't respond. The boy came down to Michael's house every morning, from where they'd walk to school together. Perpetual knew who would be at the door because her queries always went unanswered. But with Mario she'd try anyway, hoping that someday he'd talk to her. Today, he had come almost half an hour earlier than usual.

'Wait, Mario baba,' she said, lifting the latch.

When Perpetual opened the door, the boy trotted into the house. There seemed to be a spring in his step, and for a change, he smiled at her.

'Michael baba is taking a bath. Go sit,' she said.

Mario plopped himself on the cane chair even as Karen and Alfred, who had seen him come in, went about their usual chores. The Coutinhos were so used to Mario's soundless presence that it never struck them as unusual that he did not speak to them. Today though, Mario had no apprehensions about treating his neighbours to some small talk.

'Good morning, aunty, good morning, uncle,' he said.

Karen, who was occupied with sewing a floral pattern on a piece of linen, stared at the boy suspiciously. She wasn't sure if she had heard him right.

'Aye, morning, son,' she said, as an afterthought.

Alfred, who was engrossed in the Bible, was also distracted momentarily. He smiled at the kid and went back to reading the Book of Psalms. Mario didn't greet them otherwise, so his thoughtful gesture left the couple perplexed.

As soon as he had made himself comfortable, Mario flashed his box at them. 'See, pai gave me,' he said.

'A new pencil set, that's lovely, men,' Karen replied. By then, Michael had come out from his bath. 'Mario, how come you are here so early?'

'Mike, see, pencils.' Mario got a pencil out of the red box and showed off the rubber tip to his friend.

'This is wonderful. Who bought?' Michael asked.

'Pai, for birthday.'

'Oh, yes! I completely forgot. Mama, it is Mario's birthday today.'

Karen figured that the birthday and the gift had breathed some life into the boy. If only every day could be like today, Mario wouldn't come across as strange, Karen thought to herself.

'How old are you now, baba?' she enquired.

'Seven,' he blushed.

'Aye, that's wonderful! Wait one minute, I shall get you some candies, huh,' she said, calling out to Perpetual to fetch the jar of sweets from the kitchen.

Sometime later, Mario returned home with a fistful of colourful peppermints and jujubes. He handed them to his mother disinterestedly and rushed to put the pencil box in his parents' almirah, only pulling out one from the set to place between the pages of his notebook. He then left for school with Michael.

It was Tresa who had requested Michael to walk her son to school every morning. It was convenient because both of them studied at the same school—St Sebastian Goan High School—which was just a few miles away from Dr D'Lima Street. That Mario only got along with Michael helped.

The boys from Cavel had to cross Chira Bazaar to reach the school. Negotiating the market's early morning bustle of tongas, crawling trams, clinking cycles and swiftly moving feet could sometimes be frightening. Your body had to act faster than your mind, so that you could steer clear of being hit by something unexpected. Michael knew of Mario's wandering mind and always held his hand tightly.

Even today, Mario was indulging in his fantasies. He was walking with Michael, but his mind was elsewhere. He was thinking of the drawing book, and how he'd go back home and draw his teacher Glenda's face. She was the only person he liked at school.

For a newly seven-year-old, he had a shockingly observant eye and a great photographic memory. The hollow of Glenda's eyes, her broad forehead and pointed nose which curved like a hook at the base were accurately embedded in his memory. He had been waiting for the right moment to draw her picture. Now that he had been given these pencils, it felt like the perfect time to start on his project.

'So what will you do with your new pencils?' Michael asked Mario, interrupting his friend's reverie.

'A face,' Mario said.

'Whose face?' Michael asked, but noticing Mario flush with embarrassment, he simply added, 'Show me once it is done, okay?'

The kid nodded.

Mario appeared more willing to engage in conversation today, so Michael kept going with more questions. That was how he assured himself that the boy wasn't the weird child that everyone said he was. 'What are you going to do for your birthday?' he asked.

But Mario had drifted off once again, and replied by half-rotating his fingers to convey that he didn't really know. Though, minutes later, he did reply, as if he himself had been trying to find an answer to Michael's question. 'I will go garden.'

It was a relatively quiet day. The afternoon sun had peaked early, enveloping Cavel in a coat of warmth. The summer of April was still bearable. It was May that was wretched and ruthless. At the Lawrences' home, preparations for a small birthday celebration were underway.

David had taken leave that Friday. He had told his son that he would pick him up from St Sebastian's in the evening but hadn't revealed his plans to take him to a nearby garden after that. It was meant to be a surprise. Tresa had already prepared the batter for baath, a Goan delicacy made with coconut and semolina. Since they didn't have an oven of their own, she had to take it to the bakery in Cross Gully, where baker Lasario Pementa, a friend of the family, would cook it in his brick oven along with other nankhatais they sold at the bakery. 'I will make the softest cake for my Mario baba,' he told her.

For dinner, Tresa planned to rustle up a scrumptious chicken stew, and even sent David to pick up broiler chicken from the market.

Around 1 p.m., while David was on his way back, he was accosted by his co-worker Dilipbhai Patel at the entrance of Pope's Colony. 'Oh, good I met you here. I was coming to your house only,' Dilipbhai said, struggling to catch his breath. 'Chalo jaldi.'

'Where?'

'To Victoria Dock.'

'What happened?'

'Arre, they saw some smoke.'

'But I am on leave.'

'What are you saying, David bhai? This is the time to fight. I heard something very bad happened there, but nobody is telling us anything. All holidays have been cancelled. My gut says that they have dropped that bomb,' Dilipbhai said, his fingers moving restlessly.

As soon as David heard that, alarm bells rang in his head.

'Wait here. I am coming,' he said.

'No, no, head directly to the station. I will meet you there.'

David had an inkling of what could have happened. He was sure that this wasn't any regular fire. If the entire squad had been asked to show up, it had to be something huge. This was wartime, and though the English had distanced Bombay from the Second World War, the threat loomed large. Rumours of

Japan sweeping down on Britain's most favoured port city via air or sea had been doing the rounds for a very long time now. The imagined attack, in fact, had become part of Bombay's paranoia. Rumours spread like wildfire in the brigade and for all their ability to douse flames, the firemen couldn't quell this one. Every day there was a new prophecy about possible bombings in Bombay.

David quickened his pace as he walked towards Bosco Mansion. As he took the wooden staircase, he couldn't rid himself of a heavy feeling that left his stomach in knots.

His job had always kept him on tenterhooks. It was like going to war. Only here, he was not fighting people, but fire. At least people were predictable. Very target oriented. They either wanted to kill you or they didn't. But fire, it didn't have a mind of its own. It just raged like a mad man, spreading rapidly and engulfing everything around it. Your only weapon was water—which was so harmless otherwise that you couldn't even trust if it would be enough to calm the fiery blaze.

David didn't speak of the dangers of his job at home as it would worry his wife. With nobody except him to fend for his family, he had wished for another life—that of a bread maker. Being a fireman, after all, was not something that he had chosen for himself. David was a victim of circumstances, both good and bad.

Orphaned as a child, twelve-year-old David had come to Bombay from the village of Parra in Goa with just ten annas in hand. He had lived in a kudd in Jer Mahal, Dhobi Talao, which he shared with fellow villagers for nearly eleven years while working at Cavel's Costa Bakery, which had opened after the unceremonious shut down of Padaria de Cavel in the 1900s, following the death of its owner.

The kudds of Bombay—chummeries started by the ingenious Goans in the mid-nineteenth century—were the mainstay of many migrants, especially the bachelors. The humble lodgings assured at least a roof above their heads, while they tottered and struggled in the new city. Run by Goan clubs, each attached to a village back home, they offered membership for just a few annas. The amenities were basic. A bed, a metal box for your clothes, and a common dining table and toilet, all crammed on one floor. But the goodwill that existed among the members compensated for everything else. Work was distributed equally—David had to share the tasks of cooking, cleaning and maintaining the quarters with the other sailors, cooks and musicians lodged at the kudd. Life here was never a bore. On weekends, there was free-flowing alcohol with chakna, music and carrom to keep them entertained. They also tided over hard times together. There was a common kitty to which they all contributed and which came to their rescue when jobs were scarce and money nil.

David's marriage to Tresa, also an orphan, had been arranged. She had been a cook with a family of Goan Bammons—the Catholic Brahmins of Goa. He had met her on the insistence of the Sisters of the Sacred Heart Children's Home in Goa which had looked after the two orphans when they were younger. He had been eighteen and she a shy fourteen-year-old when they tied the knot.

But he had had no plans to bring Tresa to Bombay; not until he found himself a home. It was a dog's life here, and if he were to bring her to the city, it had to be worth it. Fortunately for him, his boss Leon Feleciano daCosta, an ailing unmarried man whose bakery David had taken care of as his own, surreptitiously transferred the tenancy rights of his house to David just before he had died.

The good news brought some bad tidings for the young man as well, because Leon's second cousin, Baptista, co-owner of Costa Bakery, could not reconcile with the fact that his relative had given away his grand home in Cavel to an absolute stranger, and worse, to someone with a dubious ancestry. Not only did he think that David was undeserving, but he also strongly felt that a man worthy of living in a kudd shouldn't be granted such a prized property. First, he fired David from the job. Next, he dragged him to court. But the foolhardy Baptista daCosta, who had accused the innocent David of brainwashing his cousin, lost the battle without a good fight. The documents were proof: Leon trusted David more than Baptista.

David's problems, however, had just begun. A year of joblessness followed with David doing menial labour, including working in a garage and selling bread from door to door in Cavel. He had become the butt of jokes in the neighbourhood, for though he had inherited a fine fortune, he was living like a pauper.

Months of hopelessness followed. In a fit of desperation, David decided to give up on the only property he had ever had to his name when he chanced upon an advertisement in the newspaper for vacancies in the Bombay Fire Brigade. Five months later, he brought Tresa to the big, bad city of Bombay—the place where some of his dreams had been broken and new ones made.

When Tresa opened the door, she sensed something amiss. But David appeared too flustered to be barraged with questions. He quickly dumped the market bag on the table and changed into his spare uniform.

It was only when he was getting ready to leave that Tresa asked, 'What?'

'Something at the docks.'

'And baba? What to tell him?'

David, who was sitting on the stool to put on his boots, locked eyes with his wife briefly before going back to the task. When he had completed it, he rested both his hands on his thighs for a few seconds and gently said, 'I will be back.'

As he rose to leave, Tresa caught hold of him and gave him a long, tight hug. She was shaking nervously. David had been in the same spot before, but it had never moved her enough to react. He responded with a firm kiss on her lips before letting her go.

She spent the rest of the afternoon preparing the chicken curry. She even went and picked up the baath from Pementa's bakery. It smelled of burnt bricks and coconut. There was still time before Mario came back from school. Tresa hoped that David would be back by early evening so that he could take their son to the garden.

At 4.40 p.m., when there was still no news from her husband, a restless Tresa went out to her balcony. The sky was an amorphous blue-grey. The compound was still—almost frozen. The trees weren't rustling; the gentle, warm afternoon breeze was long dead. She stood there for a while and then went back to the kitchen to boil milk for her son, who was going to be home soon.

Barely had she placed the vessel on the kerosene stove when the floor beneath her shook with such determined force that it threw her to the ground. A huge deafening sound followed, numbing her ears for a few grave minutes. Even months after she recovered from the impact, Tresa could still not decide what had been more terrifying—the explosion that had rattled the very foundation of her kitchen or the ear-splitting noise that came with it.

At school, Mario had already packed his bag. He was holding onto his pencil, waiting for the closing bell, when instead of the jingling ring, a loud thud alarmed the children. Everyone ran helter-skelter, including the teachers, who for a change had absolutely no control over their students.

A peon screamed, 'We have been bombed. The Japani have bombed us.'

Everyone thought this to be a fact. Michael, whose classroom was two floors above Mario's, scampered down to get the boy so that he could take him home safely. To his luck, Mario was waiting outside his class even as the rest of the kids were making a dash for the exit. Tears were rolling down the boy's cheeks.

'Shush, don't cry. I am taking you home. Let's go.'

'Pai,' Mario asked between sobs, 'Where is pai?'

'He must be at home, waiting for you. Let us go.'

'No, pai taking me home.'

'Mario, no time to argue, we have to go.'

'No,' he said, his hands shaking uncontrollably.

'Mario, please understand. If you don't come with me now, your father will get worried.'

After much persuasion, Mario reached for Michael's hand and the two ran out of school.

Outside, the sky had turned a bright orange as if the sun had exploded and melded into the blue. Bombay was burning. Smoke engulfed Chira Bazaar, tormenting the cotton clouds.

The duo juggled their way through the busy by-lane that opened onto the main road. A sea of people spilt onto the road with little direction, looking for a haven that would shield them from the over-lit, smoky sky. The word 'bomb' was oft-repeated by the harrowed crowd. A thundering explosion could once again be heard somewhere in the distance. 'Another bomb,' someone yelled.

Michael had broken into a cold sweat and his clammy palm was losing grip of Mario's hand even as the kid tried hard to hold on. They were struggling to make their way forward, when they bumped into Perpetual.

'Thank God, Oh, Jesus! Oh, Mother Mary! Thank God. You boys safe,' the maid blurted out. 'Come! Come! We go home.'

She placed her heavy arms on their lean shoulders, leading them through the terror-stricken crowd. It was only when they were halfway home that Mario realised his pencil had disappeared from his hands.

'My pencil,' he cried. 'I lost pencil.'

His eyes turned moist. 'I want pencil,' he said, and collapsed onto the ground, determined not to go on.

Perpetual and Michael had no idea why the pencil meant so much to him.

'We have to go, Mario baba. We will come back to look for it.'

But Mario wouldn't stir. The two had to lug him home, dragging him through the maddened crowd.

Pope's Colony was in a state of panic too. Everyone—the Coutinhos, D'Limas, Crastos, da Cunhas, D'Souzas and D'Costas—had made their way to the compound. They didn't have the courage to step out of their colony but hovered around the gate to make sense of what was happening.

Karen and her husband Alfred, who had returned early from his workplace in Ballard Estate after he had heard of some steamer catching fire at the dock nearby, were very anxious. They had sent Perpetual to fetch the boys but were appalled that Tresa and David had not even shown concern. It was only when Tresa emerged sometime after the second explosion that they realised she had been injured. She was a relatively tall woman—her narrow waist and long, slender hands accentuated her height. She was wearing a collared dress, one that she had worn two Christmases ago to mass, and her hair was tied in a neat pleat. The colour of her outfit was the same disconcerting shade as the sky. She had dressed with the hope that she would accompany David and her son to the garden.

Her arms were closely locked to her chest, her fingers clutching the elbow of her right arm.

'What happened?' Karen enquired.

'My arm broke.' Tresa was barely audible. The shouting and crying on the road drowned her voice. 'Where Michael baba and Mario?' she asked, worried.

'Perpetual has gone to bring the boys. Don't worry,' Alfred said. 'Are you okay?' he added.

'Uh … kitchen floor shake and I fall down,' Tresa said. She was struggling with her English, but she tried.

'Aye. Even I fell off the bed with a thud, men,' Karen said. 'God knows what happened. I hope it's not the Japanese.'

'Where is David? Wasn't he on holiday?' Alfred asked, noticing suddenly that Tresa had come down alone.

'He go to Victoria Dock.'

'Oh no!' Alfred said. He seemed worried.

'Why?' she asked.

He said nothing.

When Mario finally came, he looked bedraggled. His white uniform had turned a dull brown. 'We had to drag him, aunty. He refused to come with us,' Michael said to Tresa, justifying the boy's messy appearance. 'I think he lost his pencil.'

Tresa gave Michael a comforting smile. 'Sorry, so much trouble, baba.'

'It is no trouble at all, aunty.'

Once they were home, Mario ran into his parent's room, and crouched in a corner, crying hysterically. Tresa went to her son, and nestled him in her embrace, though her arm hurt badly.

'What happen, baba? No scared, okay?'

'Pencil,' he cried, 'I lost.'

'You have more, na. Pai no getting angry.'

'Where pai?' Mario asked, between sobs.

'He coming. He gone out.'

'I have gift for pai,' Mario said.

'Arre … nice. What you got?' Tresa asked curiously.

Mario opened the flap of his khadi bag and took out a notebook. On the last page of the book, he had sketched the face of the man who had made his morning sparkle.

Tresa moved her delicate fingers on the thin sheet of paper. She observed the features closely. The round eyes partly rimmed by the thick eyebrows, the chiselled jaw-line that led to the handsome cleft chin, and the prominent cupid's bow of the lips veiled by the handlebar moustache that had brushed against her lips earlier in the day. How beautiful he is, she thought.

Three days later, while pensively staring at the same sketch, her yearning for her husband would manifold into a kind of desperation that she found extremely hard to reveal.

'When pai come?' Mario asked her again.

'Very soon, baba, very soon,' Tresa repeated calmly. The stoic expression on her face was unnerving and paralysing at the same time.

5

THE WEDDING AT CAVEL

November 1953

The bell at the Church of Our Lady of Hope swung slowly, ringing a sound so beautiful that those who heard it wouldn't forget it for aeons. It had music, it had rhythm and it had strength. It had everything a church bell could boast of; such was the sway of the enormous clapper that when it struck the rim of its brass container, its thud pervaded through all of Cavel in a divine, ceremonious hum.

A recent addition to the two-hundred-and-thirty-five-year-old church—after the last bell had died a painful death when it accidentally fell off the frame and was crushed beyond recognition—this instrument played for the first time at Michael Coutinho and Merlyn Ermelinda Mascarenhas' wedding.

The new bell was a restored eighteenth-century war-time relic from the Battle of Bassein, now Vasai, a suburban town nearly seventy kilometres from Bombay. In the 1730s, when the Marathas decided to wage war against the Portuguese who helmed Bassein, they first started by conquering their territories and forts in the vicinity. By the time the Portuguese surrendered in Bassein, the Marathas had already destroyed eighty churches, including those in Chaul, Daman and Diu, and Revdanda. The bell now sitting in Cavel had been given as a gift to one of the Maratha army officials as a victory symbol from that war. After ringing at a temple in Raigad for over two and a half centuries, a sarpanch of the village noticed the crucifix embossed on it and decided to return it to the church. It travelled over eighty-five kilometres to the Archdiocese of Bombay, where it was repaired and refurbished to its former glory. After deliberations, the priests decided that the church at Cavel should be the rightful recipient of this ancient instrument, because its own history was so closely enmeshed with a Portuguese feudal lord who had once owned the chapel. That said, nobody had been able as yet to accurately confirm the ancestry of the bell. Its 'history' was all conjecture.

'We have a surprise for you,' Fr Augustine Fernandez, the priest officiating at the wedding, said to the newly married couple after they had taken their vows. Michael and Merlyn were in the midst of unriddling the priest's cryptic declaration when the bell suddenly chimed. The groom broke into a happy smile. The bride blushed. The congregation listened with rapt attention. On Dr D'Lima Street, passers-by stopped in their places to listen to it.

In Cavel and the many churches nearby, it was a time-honoured tradition to ring the bell daily at dawn. If the bell rang at any other time, it was either to announce the death of a parishioner or to make known that the sacrament of matrimony had just been bestowed upon a couple. Today, it rang only for happy reasons.

The sweet-sounding bell worked its magic on Merlyn in particular. Still far from polishing her apologetic English, Merlyn was aware that the elite Cavelites would try and make conversation with her today. Her fear was that she would give herself away and that she'd be mocked for landing such a good catch—a writer husband, who spoke impeccable English. She was aware that even her in-laws, especially her mum-in-law, Karen, joked about how she was an embarrassment to the Goans. While Michael had been encouraging, it was only the harmonious music from the bell that calmed her anxious nerves.

On that wintry day of 15 November 1953, when the wedding party was still reeling from the aftereffects of that resounding church bell, the Goan Catholic Club at Pius House, where the reception was to take place, was also swept off its foundations by the sound.

With a guest list of over five hundred people, boundless food and wine, and a live band to keep all and sundry occupied, the wedding was expected to be the grandest Cavel and its neighbouring Catholic hamlets had ever witnessed.

The icing on the cake was the arrival of a heavyweight guest, who was the subject of discussion even before the wedding invitations were out. Anxious mothers and loveless daughters had never waited so eagerly to receive an invitation to the reception as they did now—all so they could feast their eyes on Merlyn's hockey-player cousin, Lester Fernandes. He was the son of her step-mum Coleen Ferreira's eldest sister.

A wink shy of making it to the Indian national hockey team, Lester, whose distinguished and charming good looks were much talked about from Colaba to Cuffe Parade, had reluctantly agreed to grace his cousin's celebration at the club. He was too proud a man to be seen among the ordinary, but the Ferreiras loved to show off the men of their family. They declared that Lester would raise the toast at the wedding. That way the Coutinhos were assured that the sports hero would be present at the function, even if for a while.

It was also common knowledge that the family was desperately looking for a wife for the twenty-nine-year-old sports hero. Lester, people said, had not once looked at a girl with the roving eye of a man hungry for female attention. Which parent would dare forego a chance to marry their daughter to a man of such fine distinction?

Families invited to the reception saw to it that their daughters were dressed as gorgeously as the bride. When the mass came to an end, you could see the pretty lasses head for the reception at Pius House. Marlene D'Silva was dressed like a canary. The yellow of her dress and the white of her shoes, accessorised with glistening pearl jewellery and imbued with the richness of the steely-grey sea, made her the brightest prospect among the gold-diggers' club. Thelma D'Costa was a close second. She was a piano virtuoso, whose gifted fingers were as much the talk of the town as Lester's hockey stick. She had turned into a fine beauty, but it was her teal-blue knee-length cotton skirt teamed with an off-white silk blouse that was the distraction today. Her only drawback was her pallid face that, despite bearing the features of a beautiful young lady, lacked the grace to warm a man's heart. Even if she smiled, you could never tell; even if she cried, you would never know. That was how plastic her face was—unmoved and non-malleable to the swings and slides of human emotions.

Michael's sister, Annette, too was making heads turn as Merlyn's dainty bridesmaid. But sound mind had prevailed for a change. All of sixteen, Annette thought herself too young to pursue her sister-in-law's 'handsomely old' cousin.

Meanwhile, Ellena Gomes was also dragged into this pantomime to forage in newer pastures. It would be abominable to roam with a sullen heart and grieve the loss of love when she was a step closer to meeting an outstanding man of great talent, Ellena's mother Giselle had told her. 'You must move on, child,' she said. 'When one door closes, another one opens. Grab hold of this Lester boy.'

Ellena wasn't stirred by her mother's persuasive spirit and however hard she tried, she would never fall in love with another man again.

At the Goan Catholic Club, chairs had been rented to accommodate the guests. Neatly arranged in four or five rows across the hall, the arrangement gave ample room for people to hit the floor and shake a leg. Five tables were closely put together at one end of the club to stock the rich buffet, which had been prepared in full earnest by the women from the Coutinho, Ferreira and Mascarenhas households. Almost all of them were still recovering from the stupor of tirelessly working overnight in their home kitchens. But the ladies knew how to put up a show of infallible elegance. If you saw them, you wouldn't say they had been overspent by the rigours of endless cooking or darkened by the soot emerging from their coal stoves.

One table had been kept aside specifically for Karen's ceramic jars that bore the fruit of her ancestral wine-making wisdom. Karen's wine had always been the most sought after in the neighbourhood, especially during Christmas. Of late, though, her neighbour Tresa had been giving her stiff competition.

In the last few months, Tresa aunty cho add'do had begun selling wine fermented to unmatched perfection. This was not the case a few years ago, when Tresa served only insipid country liquor to her customers, making her drinking stable very unpopular in Chira Bazaar. Thank God for the lady's ingenuity; her homemade wine and the bangda (mackerel) fry stuffed with recheado masala came to her rescue and helped her keep her dhando afloat.

The bangda fry was tedious to prepare. First, Tresa had to clean the innards of the mackerel, and then slit it horizontally from both sides before stuffing it with the recheado, which she made using dry Kashmiri chilli, vinegar, a pinch of sugar, garlic, ginger and a combination of spices picked up from the recipe book of the family in Goa, where she had worked as a maid for several years. She squeezed a dash of lemon over it, serving it hot out of the frying pan. Her wines ranged from beetroot, rice and ginger to the fruitier options like grape, pineapple and orange.

But the rivalry to produce the best wine in Cavel really had nothing to do with why Karen had left out Tresa's name from the guest list today. Despite Michael's insistence on having Mario's mother at his wedding, the senior Coutinhos had maintained that inviting a lady who made a living by drowning men in the terrible vice of alcohol would tarnish the reputation that their family had so carefully nurtured. Even if she were driven to terrible circumstances following her husband's death, she shouldn't have chosen this line to keep her home running, Karen had argued.

'Aye, this lady is spoiling our name, men. Staying in Bosco and making daaru. One day the pandus will pick her up and throw her in jail. Chee. That David died with honour and see his wife,' she had said.

David Lawrence had died a hero on 14 April 1944, when the freighter SS Fort Stikine—carrying a highly inflammable cargo of cotton bales, one million pounds sterling in gold ingots, and around twelve hundred tonnes of explosives— that had arrived from Karachi a day earlier and was stationed at Bombay's Victoria Dock No. 1, caught fire, leading to two shattering explosions. Around thirteen hundred people who lived in the vicinity of the harbour, were killed. Of these, sixty-six were firemen. Over eighty thousand people were rendered homeless. The British-Indian censors relayed the true story behind the events of the day only a month later.

Needless to say, Tresa was ostracised by the rest of her neighbours too. That did not stop the men of Cavel—even those who never approved of her business—from making a pitstop at her joint. When they arrived at the add'do, their pretence would at once cease with the smell of alcohol. They'd drink their troubles down and pour out their worries to the same woman who, in the outside world, they made a show of hating. They hoped she would understand. And for some reason, she actually did. Because to Tresa, these men were not just her customers, but also her prodigal fathers, brothers and sons. They only kept up their act of contempt to please their wives and mothers. As long as they knew when to get rid of their masks and reach out to the reality that Tresa's nest promised, it did not affect her.

By early noon, all the guests had made themselves comfortable in the club, except for one. The sports star strutted into the hall just a few minutes before the wedding entourage was expected to show up. A pin-drop silence followed, and then a collective sigh. The excitement at the club was palpable. It was amusing how the crowd reacted together like a flock of geese, experiencing the same crazy turbulence, sparked by their fantasies.

Lester was devastatingly handsome and nobody in the hall could deny this. He was broad-shouldered, with the bulk of his chest, chiselled arms and slim waist revealed from within his fitted turtleneck shirt, making him look nothing short of a Greek God. The good looks were an added bonus, especially the pointed nose that gave his face the sharp edge that could stir unholy cravings within women. Having deliberately delayed his entry to avoid becoming the centre of attention, Lester dragged up a chair and sat in a corner, next to the table of half-full wine glasses, beyond everybody's line of vision. Here, he hoped he could hide from the prying eyes of leering young girls and older women.

A musical bell, great wine and most importantly, an eligible bachelor—this celebration had all the ingredients to turn out an excellent dish. But alas, what can be said of anything that holds great promise? Can it ever match up to the aromas that teased your taste buds?

Sometime after Lester entered the hall and Michael and Merlyn started walking up the stairs of Pius House, the bell struck once again, this time without good reason.

Days later, when the priest questioned the bell-keeper about it, he apologised profusely for getting carried away by its music. 'I was tempted to strike it again,' he said.

Unfortunately, bigger apologies were in the offing because when the bell echoed through the lanes and by-lanes of Cavel again, Pius House, which was already on shaky ground, was directly hit by the bullet of its sound. Blame it on the weak foundation of the century-old stone structure or its inability to carry the weight of humanity that had poured all at once into its den, but the building started vibrating.

The couple and their party of best men and bridesmaids, who were still walking up the stairs of the building, paused for a moment. The crowd gathered at the Goan Club also felt their chairs rattle. But the tremor barely lasted for a couple of seconds, and nobody thought it significant enough to ponder upon. The guests continued to busy themselves with merriment, unperturbed by what they had just experienced. Yet, faint murmurs were audible.

'Did you just feel the ground shake? Or was it something I imagined?'

This moment of disquieting calm wouldn't last long. Less than a minute after the building exposed its vulnerability, a violent thump followed by the thunderous sound of crashing glasses and the breaking of something rock solid sent the crowd into an absolute frenzy.

Then, out of the blue, Thelma D'Costa screeched out loud as if her heart had just been pierced with a sharp dagger.

'He's gone! He's gone!' she cried desperately.

'Who?' somebody asked.

Her panic-stricken face turned towards where the table with the glasses of wine and the ceramic jars had once been placed. There was nothing there anymore. No table. No wine. No jars. And no Lester either. Instead, there was a gaping hole so wide that everyone's eyes widened in horror. Part of the floor of the Goan Catholic Club had just caved in, and it had taken along with it the best part of this celebration.

Everybody knew where Lester was, but they feared going close, worried that the rest of the floor would also split apart. They all scrambled towards the only door in the hall in the hope of saving their own skin.

Amidst this chaos, one of the guests stopped Michael and Merlyn, who had almost made it to the club, and told them what had happened. Their immediate concern was obviously Lester. The hockey player had fallen into the spacious flat owned by the Fernandes family, who had vacated the house a few years earlier when they shifted to a bungalow in Bandra. Michael immediately rushed to the floor below the club. A heavy brass lock held the wooden door in its place; it would take a few more men than Michael to break it open. After a few strikes of a hammer and saw, they finally managed to make it inside.

The room where the ceiling had caved in was a mess. Shards of glass and broken ceramic pieces were lying alongside scattered bricks of concrete, all of which were faintly dyed in the red of the wine that was now snaking out from the debris. Fortunately, two broken planks of wood had fallen over the rubble and shielded Lester from grave damage. He was sandwiched between the planks, caked in dust and bleeding profusely. It was hard to tell what was wine and what blood. But somebody was already down there, cleaning his wounds with a piece of cloth torn from her teal-blue skirt. The sight was bitter-sweet.

Thelma's daredevilry could put any man to shame. She had jumped into the cavity to rescue Lester, unconcerned about the harm she would be putting herself to. The gap between the ceiling and the floor wasn't huge, and so, apart from a few minor gashes, Thelma barely had any injuries at all.

Lester, however, looked like he had suffered many a broken bone and had to be taken to the nearby Bombay Hospital. He was breathing, talking, and surprisingly, smiling. And maybe he was already in love. Why else would he insist that only Thelma accompany him?

As the injured Lester was being rushed to the hospital in the ambulance, the guests gathered at the compound of Bosco Mansion pondered upon their fate. Would there be a celebration, or if not, would they at least get some food and wine?

The Mascarenhas were, however, quick with their planning and decided to shift the venue to their villa in Girgaum. The band's instruments and the food were still lying at the Goan Club, because apart from the huge chunk of flooring that had taken Lester and the wine down, everything else was left intact and undisturbed. But the building was vacated and nobody was allowed to enter until the firemen showed up.

Karen, though, was still in shock. She was wallowing in the grief of losing wine that had taken three long months of relentless fermenting and straining. It had drained into the debris and sweetened Lester's pain, but there was no telling how much hurt and humiliation it caused Karen.

'How can you have a wedding without wine? This is a bad omen,' she overheard one of her Rosario sisters say. 'Call off the wedding! I always told you that Merlyn is not good enough for our Mike,' another one said.

Her husband and the Mascarenhas family were more understanding of her plight. With Prohibition tightening the screws on the sale of alcohol in the city, it was next to impossible to procure wine at such short notice.

'Somebody broke some bones, and we lost some good wine … that is all. Just thank God it didn't get any worse. Everyone is alive. We will still feast and dance,' Alfred said to placate Karen. 'We will toast with cola,' Michael said.

An hour later, the guests were making their way to Ferriera House, a flashy home near the small village of Khotachi Wadi, hidden in the busy market area of Girgaum. Freshly painted in a deep colour of mustard, the house was veiled with Mangalore tiles and embellished with white doors, bringing Goa alive in the south of Bombay. Apart from its airy and wide rooms, it also boasted a sprawling garden full of chiku and jackfruit trees and a stable that had now been converted into a storage house.

Unfortunately, despite the magnanimity of Merlyn's family, not everybody could be accommodated here. The band was asked to leave, but only after they were paid for their unsung labour. To make up for the lack of music, Merlyn's father shifted his wife's gramophone to the centre of the drawing room.

But a Goan wedding without a toastmaster and wine is as good as a Goan wedding without a bride and groom. It took some coaxing before Michael's groomsman Joe Crasto agreed to raise the toast. 'I will keep it very short. You know how nervous I get when I have to speak in front of people,' he told Michael. The fact that he had agreed to raise the toast was reassuring enough for Michael, who was still reeling from the wreck that this celebration had been through.

For now, he was glad that his bride wasn't panicking like his mother. Merlyn had been sincerely composed through the drama. Despite her cousin having taken a beating in the mess, she did not let it show. Merlyn would later claim that the bell had done the trick, leaving her in a trance for days. The irony of her misplaced love for a bell that had single-handedly spearheaded the destruction of her wedding reception wasn't lost on Michael.

––

It was 2.30 p.m. by the time the gathering settled into the simple comforts of the home reception. All the doors and windows were left open to allow the flow of light and air so that the place didn't feel claustrophobic. The guests occupied every inch of space inside the many rooms of the house as well as the garden, where wooden chairs—borrowed from neighbouring villas—kept the tired and restless comfortably glued and numb.

This celebration was already moving in no particular order. A typical Goan wedding reception wouldn't have begun before the toast. But the guests were so famished that the hosts decided otherwise. Wafers and cutlets were being distributed plate by plate—both the families had ensured that they were generously stocked in that department. A handful of men and women took to the floor of the drawing room, jiving to music that played on the gramophone. The music wasn't loud enough to liven up the occasion, but it kept everyone light and merry on their feet.

Annette, who thought herself the most striking beauty in the crowd, tried to seek the attention of many a man. She even flirted with Michael's groomsman, Joe Crasto, from whom she was taking guitar lessons, and teased him like a schoolgirl when he confessed that he had two left feet and wouldn't be able to dance with her.

'What kind of man says no to a gorgeous girl like me?'

Joe threw her an amused look. He was still annoyed with her for causing gashes on the fretboard of his guitar.

'A man who loves his guitar too much,' he sneered. 'Also, I am preparing for my speech right now, Annette. So please go disturb somebody else.'

'Uff! You are such a bore, Joe. No wonder you have no girlfriend.'

Joe took the jibe personally. He would have continued to argue with her, but Benjamin da Cunha swooped in on them, like a watchful hawk, and swung Annette to the floor, looping her arms around him as they glided to a jive number. Benjamin may not have had the confidence to talk to her, but he could still win her over with his dancing skills.

It was here that he took a not-so-innocent chance and grabbed her buttocks to pull her close to his body so that she could feel how his manhood swelled for her. Her body lingered against his for a few seconds, but Annette instantly pulled herself away. She stayed for another dance, however, unsure if the discomfort she had just experienced had been an accident or the intentional doing of a wild heart. A few years later, on the day of her own engagement, the strange stirrings she felt when their bodies pressed against each other would race through her mind and entrap her.

When the bride and groom primped themselves up, Joe Crasto took centre-stage in the garden. The Mascarenhases got their servants to distribute glasses of cola to everybody present. The male guests stood up grudgingly to keep up the show of a toast that really wasn't.

Joe's speech was to be brief. He kept re-reading the paper on which he had written the line that he found so difficult to memorise. 'I love my friend Michael and wish him a very happy married life' was all he planned to say before raising his glass to toast the wedding. Public speeches were definitely not his cup of tea.

But when Joe got out there, nervously stuttered that line aloud and took a sip of the cola, something unbelievable happened. All the guests who had taken a swig of the soft drink right after him felt the same unexplainable energy.

To convince himself, Joe took another sip and then gulped down the whole glass. 'I haven't finished,' he informed the guests. 'There is so much more I have to say about my dear friend Michael and his wonderful wife Merlyn ...' And Joe went on for the next fifteen minutes, unruffled by the number of people staring at him while listening to him share amusing vignettes about the couple.

This was the day when the seeds of 'the superstar' were first sown in Joe. From managing a classy and confident toast at Michael's wedding to becoming a rising music artist, this was going to be a journey that none had predicted for the lad.

Michael was stunned by what he saw. Everyone was so jubilant and content. The mishaps from early that afternoon seemed to have all been forgotten. He had been so exhausted that he hadn't bothered to drink to his own toast. But the party was fuelled with a sense of joie de vivre that was so infectious that he eventually did place his mouth to the glass. And when he did, he couldn't stop drinking. He looked at his wife, who shared the same confused but relieved expression, unlike his mother. Karen seemed irritated after sipping the drink.

And then it struck Michael that she should have been here too. He scanned the sea of people for her face. A woman of her height could definitely not have gone unnoticed. His eyes jumped quickly past the happy faces of men and women who were downing the cola with surprising relish, until he found her standing against a wall. She had been watching him all along, with the anxiety of a woman wanting to please.

She was the same woman who was rejected by many. But today, if not for her timely intervention, this party wouldn't be redeemed from the same scorn and disdain that kept her away from the people she had once thought to be her own.

Michael got hold of another glass from the tray that was doing the rounds. This time, he toasted Jesus and regaled the crowd with the story of Christ's first miracle at the wedding at Cana. '… and thus, it goes that he transformed water into wine,' Michael said as he ended his story, before winking at aunty Tresa.

She returned his gesture with a knowing smile, her eyes glinting with joy. In his silence, he had communicated a promise: he would always be grateful.

6

A FRIEND CALLED JOE

September 1972

It was past 3 a.m. when Rose Maria Crasto woke from her slumber. She switched on the electric light at her bedside, but couldn't distinguish grey from black. The room was still pitch dark; the faint red glow that created a mystical halo around the small bulb on the side table didn't reveal anything except for the warmth of colour. She switched it off and went back to sleep. Had she known that her husband wasn't in the room, she wouldn't have been fooled by the peace of that night. But Rose assumed that Joe had been with her all along. Truly, the night reveals nothing. Not sorrow. Not joy. It only ferments dreams. And in her dreams, Joe was sleeping by her side, with his head resting on the palm of her left hand. She sang him a song and lulled him to sleep. And they lived happily ever after.

Who would have thought that Joe Crasto, Michael Coutinho's best friend and the star singer of the Catholic Gymkhana, would return to the very same building that had housed all his miseries? It was a fact that Joe's marriage to

Rose Maria—the sole heiress of an eighteen-hundred-square-foot home on the ground-floor of Bosco Mansion—had been a matter of settling old scores.

Fourteen years his senior, Rose Maria, the widow of architect Gerard D'Costa, was wooed into love. So madly had she fallen for the singer that better sense had failed to prevail. That she was fifty-four and he forty had gnawed at her in the beginning, but Joe managed to quell those misgivings.

'What will our relatives think?' she had asked when Joe broached marriage.

'My brothers and sisters are too busy raising their kids to care about me. And you'd know about your family more than I will. But think about it. Have they even bothered to keep in touch with you after Gerard passed away? See, Rose, we have a chance to start again. We got lucky; we found each other. I am not going to force you to marry me, but I can promise you one thing. If you do say yes, I will do everything I can to make this work,' he said persuasively.

Rose Maria paused to reflect on what he had said. She was infatuated with him, but as soon as you added numbers to their relationship, it felt like a botched-up sum. No formula could help crack it. 'Joe, if only I had been born twenty years later, we would still stand a chance,' she said.

The two went back and forth for a while. But one afternoon in May 1969, under the sweltering blanket of Bombay's summer, when Joe had filled her with his hard and unyielding manhood, arousing her dormant sex, she knew that this was all she had longed for since her husband had died, uncoupling her from one of the sweetest pleasures of life. This physicality had been so intense that it stirred her to change her mind overnight. She married Joe a few days later, and her bed flourished again with lust and love. For her, it was equal parts of both. To Joe, it meant nothing at all.

Over a decade earlier, when Annette had eloped with Benjamin on her birthday, returning as a married woman, Joe's life had been blown to smithereens.

His mind turned into a wasteland, occupied vacuously by thoughts of the fiancée who had abandoned him. He wouldn't eat a morsel of food, not even his favourite bhendi aani sungta chi kuddy (okra-prawn curry) that his sister-in-law prepared daily for nearly a month, in the hope that he'd put an end to this starvation. But all he wanted to do was wallow in his grief. Each morning when he woke up, the haunting image of Annette walking out of the Goan Catholic Club with a smashed Benjamin would cripple his senses. During this time, he also suffered a professional setback. Unable to think straight, he had turned down the contract to perform with the band at the Taj Mahal Palace Hotel. The lover got his comeuppance for doing nothing but loving.

He felt alive only when he was fast asleep or after downing the many neat pegs of aunty Tresa's country liquor, which brought on that sleep. But Joe's drunken sprees were so damaging that his family feared he was becoming a bad influence on his young nieces and nephews, all of whom lived in the same house.

That's how he found himself a bed at the dormitory of the Young Men's Christian Association (YMCA) on Lamington Road, two bus stops from D'Lima Street.

Michael tried convincing his friend to move someplace else, possibly to another country. Of late, people were going to Oman and Kuwait in droves. Maybe the distance would do him some good. He was worried that living in such close proximity to D'Lima Street would not help Joe heal. He saw Joe deteriorate with each passing day, even as his sister revelled in the joys of her girlish fantasies, indifferent to the pain of her ex-fiancé.

Not once did Annette bother to ask her brother the questions that should have plagued the mind of any lover, present or past.

'Is Joe doing well?' 'Has he taken this very badly?' 'How can I help?' 'I am sorry.' 'It was a mistake.' No, none of those words was said. No apologies. No regrets.

Instead of being remorseful, Annette escaped to Goa with Benjamin for a few weeks and only returned when her parents forgave their prodigal daughter for the public humiliation.

Annette was certain that her parents would not hold a grudge against her for too long; this was but what her mama had always wished.

'Mama, you were right! Benji is the true love of my life. Only mothers know what is good for their daughters. I am sorry for not listening to you earlier,' she said, trying to massage her mum's ego.

It was easy-breezy. 'Aye, my baby has become a woman. Come give your mama a hug, men,' her mum responded, teary-eyed. All this drama made Michael sick to the pit of his stomach.

The mother and daughter turned to the new chapter very quickly. They forgot that they were characters in a novel, not a short story. In this novel, every chapter was connected to the others. And retribution was not too far away.

Alfred was on Michael's side. He hadn't yet recovered from the repulsive pelvic thrusts that Benjamin had shown off in the name of dance moves. After he learnt that his daughter had married Benjamin in Goa, he had had a moment too many of imagining a naked Benjamin dancing to *Blue Suede Shoes* in front of his daughter. When this happened, he would run to the kitchen and splash cold water on his face. It would freeze the thoughts for a few seconds before the unforgivable thrusts addled his mind again.

Benjamin da Cunha's family, who lived in Lobo Mansion, the building sharing a compound with Bosco, warmed to Karen immediately. They knew how much Benji himself had wanted this. But the da Cunhas were already a big family, and their flat was bursting at the seams with four brothers, their wives and their children. The space crunch led Benjamin, the fifth and youngest, to station himself with his in-laws. The arrival of this new crazy member of the family hastened Michael's plans of finding a new house for himself and his immediate family.

The D'Limas' flat had been on Michael's mind for a very long time. It held a lot of memories of the girl who had once taught him to drink in the small joys of rain. He wrote to Tracey's mother in Goa, and she gave him her word that the flat would be his, allaying all his fears of the D'Limas giving their home to a rich Goan buyer. That the landlord of Bosco Mansion didn't allow the tenants to transfer the rights to anyone outside the community meant that several lucrative options were closed for Linda in any case.

'I am doing this just for my Tracey,' Linda assured Michael in a letter. 'She would have wanted you to have this home.

Perhaps, if she were alive, you wouldn't even have had to buy it from me,' Linda wrote, hinting about a union that she had found unfavourable during Tracey's lifetime.

But Linda was up to her old chicanery, only trying to trap Michael into an emotional decision. After all that sugary talk, she told him that he could have her tenancy rights for a sum of seventy thousand rupees. It was a huge amount for a man who earned the meagre salary of six hundred rupees per month at *The Express* newspaper. But the shrewd and hard-hearted Linda knew that Michael would buy that flat even if it meant putting himself at financial risk. If she was destined to become rich because some foolish man was still obsessed with her dead daughter, she didn't mind waiting till eternity.

After Joe moved to Lamington Road, Michael's concerns only grew. In between managing his job, running a family and gathering funds to buy a new home, he busied himself in a mission to keep Joe at a distance from Cavel. He was partly successful.

The first task was to wean Joe off alcohol. The bait was Meryln's masala tea. For an extra salary of five rupees, Michael's maid would deliver a flask of the tea at Joe's dorm every morning, before he could wake up and take a swig of his country liquor. The alcohol didn't stand a chance against well-brewed chai.

When there was a vacancy for a guitarist at a hotel in Churchgate, it was Michael who accompanied Joe to the trials. Joe got the job at the first strum. The two became very tight after that.

There were no invitations to D'Lima Street though, not even when Michael finally bought the house on the ground-floor opposite Rose Maria's apartment. Joe was even more conspicuous by his absence at the housewarming party.

They hung out instead at Joe's aunt Lucy's place in Sonapur Galli every Sunday afternoon, where they would discuss music, food and Joe's numerous flings. Over time, Joe turned into a serial dater, breaking many hearts on his way. Annette was never mentioned in these conversations.

Time heals the broken. Sometimes, the healing is slow. Sometimes, it is slower. You cannot predict how long it will take before one forgets what it all felt like—heartbreak, the pain, the anguish, and that emptiness. Years could roll by, and you'd have done ten million different things to keep yourself from thinking, and yet, the mind would remember that moment when your life fell apart and crushed you whole.

Then one day, while lying on your bed, the fan whirring above you in circles, you'd try and dredge up that old feeling, simply out of boredom, but find you couldn't. Joe was almost there. Maybe.

Meanwhile, at the Coutinho household, the Beatles and the Jackson 5 had started giving company to Benjamin and his bottle. Benjamin found no use for his skills; the strings of the banjo, as brilliant as they were, could not be employed in a band. The failure was reinforced when he started working as a bank clerk, keeping records of accounts, loans and god knows what, but all so poorly that he should have been thankful that he had the job if not a promotion. He rewarded his incompetence with alcohol, which stoked the mindless work of his hands as he assaulted his wife. Alfred Coutinho died a sad man, just a few months shy of sixty, of a massive cardiac arrest. He had seen his daughter being thrashed in his own house by his drunk son-in-law, and it had affected him badly.

Michael had insulated himself from the madness in the house above his. The sounds of the quick movement of feet and the slamming of furniture escaped the floorboards of his parents' home into his own home very often. He never intervened.

When Annette, who had struggled to become a mother for nearly ten years, announced that she had conceived, Michael hoped that this added responsibility would save the couple. Sixty-five-year-old Karen, whose cerebral functions had taken a beating with the early onset of dementia, proclaimed that her dead husband, Alfred, was coming home again.

'Nobody is there to fight with him in heaven,' she claimed. 'I told that man not to leave without me. See now what happened, men. He is coming back as my grandchild.'

Amidst the multiple tragedies that had struck the Coutinhos, Michael's sister's pregnancy came as a silver lining.

But one night, in Annette's seventh month of pregnancy, while she was dragging her drunk husband from the sofa to their bedroom, she lost her balance and landed face down on her stomach. Michael rushed her to Bombay Hospital, but the child could not be saved.

That was the first time in many years that a troubled Michael opened up to his best friend about Annette's disastrous marriage. It was, of course, an unwise move on Michael's part because suddenly, everything Joe had forgotten beneath the whirr of that fan came rushing back to him. Joe didn't say it, but he took it upon himself to rescue his lost love from clutches of an imbecile.

Not very long after that, Joe started making trips to Bosco Mansion. In the beginning, Michael didn't think much of it and would entertain his friend at his ground-floor residence almost every weekend. But when Joe began making brief trips to see Annette on the pretext of meeting the ailing Karen, Merlyn warned her husband that nothing good was going to come of it.

One afternoon, a frightened Annette came rushing down to call her brother.

'Come up, quick,' she said, agitated.

'Is it another one of mama's bouts?' Michael enquired.

'No, no, Joe is trying to strangle Benji. He will kill him, baba.'

Michael arrived just in time to secure an inebriated Benjamin from his executioner's hands. Apparently, when Benjamin had strutted into the house after his evening fix at the Kit Kat bar near Metro Cinema and saw Joe lounging on his sofa, he had thrown a huge fit. After yelling cuss words at his nemesis, he called out to Annette, who he learnt was making rotis for Joe in the kitchen. Appalled, he hit her hard in front of her ex-fiancé. Unable to tolerate the intoxicated impudence, Joe reached for Benjamin and, sealing his fingers around his neck, swore to kill him. Had Michael arrived a few minutes later, Benjamin would probably have been in the mortuary and Joe rotting at the police station.

That evening, Michael and Merlyn sat Joe down and requested him to keep away from Cavel. They didn't realise that they were shouting in the middle of the ocean. Two weeks later, their friend was gallivanting in their compound, cooing sweet nothings into Rose Maria's ears as she watered the plants in her garden.

The next thing they knew, he was helping Rose Maria with her garden, trimming the branches and clearing the fallen leaves. Both angry and irritated, Michael refrained from exchanging anything beyond regular pleasantries with his friend.

Then one Sunday evening, Joe caught Michael off-guard when he arrived at the Coutinhos' door.

'I thought you had made a new best friend,' Michael told him sarcastically.

'Will you not ask me to come in? Is it that bad between us now?' Joe asked, as he waited patiently in the passage.

'Ryan and Sarah have their exams tomorrow, so maybe another day, Joe?' Michael said, 'You anyway seem to be spending more time here.'

'It's okay, Michael. You don't have to lie to me, I understand. But I just wanted to share a piece of news with you before it got around the parish.'

'What news?'

'I am getting married to Rose next month.'

Michael lost his bearings. It was as if somebody had sucked out a mouthful of air from his lungs and shoved it back inside immediately, stopping his breathing for a few seconds.

He dragged his friend inside and pulled him into the drawing room, where Merlyn was busy teaching the children.

'Are you out of your mind?' he yelled.

'No, not at all. I am doing what I think is right.'

'But you don't even love her.'

'That's not true.'

'Stop lying to me, you fool.' Michael's decibel levels could have shattered glass.

Merlyn and the children stared awkwardly, not sure whether it was right to stay put. Michael understood his wife's predicament and raised his eyebrows, hinting to her to leave. Merlyn took the kids to the bedroom and locked the door behind her.

'You don't love her,' Michael continued as soon as his family had left.

'Mike, I slept with her yesterday afternoon,' Joe said softly.

Michael turned red. 'I didn't have to know that.'

'You are my best friend. You are supposed to know everything about me.'

'So you're marrying her because you slept with her?'

'No, in fact, I slept with her so I could marry her.'

'Why are you doing this, Joe?' Michael asked.

'What do you mean? Aren't you happy that I am finally settling down? I know you are jealous. You can't believe that I could land myself such a good catch, isn't it so, Mike?'

'Whom are you doing this for?' Michael asked again, ignoring the rant.

'What kind of question …' Joe bit his lips in frustration. His eyes were fixed on his friend's. He knew that Michael knew, and that it would be impossible to keep up the farce anymore.

He muttered her name under his breath and stormed out. Before he left the house, he once again said the name aloud. If it had been repeated for dramatic effect, Michael couldn't tell, but irreparable damage had been done. Joe was either losing his mind or plotting something more sinister. Either way, Michael realised that forty-year-old Joe Crasto had jumped into a pit that nobody could pull him out of anymore.

After that argument, Michael chose to give Joe the silent treatment. He even skipped Joe's nuptials in church.

From being best friends to almost becoming brothers-in-law and now neighbours living on either side of the ground floor, Michael and Joe's friendship had witnessed three lives in one short lifetime of just over twenty-four years.

For once, Michael and Joe were within touching distance of each other. But never had they been so very, very distant.

Each afternoon when Michael left for work, he would see Joe attend to Rose Maria's garden. He appeared to be obsessively engaged in cleaning each and every leaf that had been soiled by layers of dust and cobwebs knitted closely by resolute spiders. Joe had given up his job at the hotel and now tutored kids at home, training them to play the guitar and the piano. He made a pittance as earnings, but having married the sole heir to such a huge house, money didn't seem like an issue of great consequence.

Almost each night was spent pleasuring Rose Maria, whom Joe had crippled and consumed with his love. Her quirks in bed—like the strange high-pitched sound she made when she was aroused, or how she would grind her teeth and keep her eyes wide open when he got himself in, her eye sockets threatening to pop out during that moment of climax—were so comical that Joe was itching to share them with Michael. But he knew his friend wouldn't entertain him anymore. Joe didn't push his luck either. The most they'd done to keep up the show of their friendship was give each other a hug after the Christmas midnight mass of 1969. The smiles they had dabbed on their faces were so forced that everyone around them could tell that something had gone wrong. While paeans are sung about lovers—the star-crossed ones and those whose stories sometimes end abruptly—of how their souls had once entwined and how they had carried inside them mirrors to each other's heart, even the best of friendships rarely inspires verse. Maybe because it's not romantic. But what is friendship, if not two people loving each other fiercely and unconditionally.

This stalemate hurt Michael greatly. He had become sluggish at work and an uninterested participant in domestic life. He was mourning the absence of his best friend. Joe was an irreplaceable piece of his heart.

The distance ruffled Joe too. But somewhere on the first floor was his lady love, for whom he had made this discomfiting comeback to D'Lima Street, and he was willing to give it his all. Anette's growing interest in him made him believe that he was on the right track.

On the sly, the two would head to the market daily, first her, and then twenty minutes later, him. They would meet at the Sonapur sabzi bazaar, where they'd plonk themselves on the parapet behind the roofed structure where hawkers lined up in rows, selling fresh veggies procured from remote Vasai and sometimes even beyond. Here, Annette would whine endlessly about her drunk husband; Joe had become her sounding board and confidante.

What was strange was that the two never spoke of their past. Annette shamelessly rattled on about how Benjamin and she had decided to get married, while behaving as if Joe had never happened to her. Only on one occasion did she hint at their shared past. While they were discussing their unhappy marriages, Annette caught Joe unawares when she asked, 'Do you miss me sometimes?'

'No,' he replied, curtly.

Joe could feel a nerve twitch within her. She had the same expression on her face as when she was upset about something.

Before she turned blue, he took her hand in his. 'Anna,' he said. 'That's such a stupid question to ask me, sweetheart, because I don't remember a moment when I stopped thinking about you.'

He drew closer to her, singing into her ears: *You were always on my mind. You were …*

She blushed.

Tell me, oh tell me … that your sweet love hasn't died.

The glint of happiness in Annette's eyes was sincere, and only Joe could tell.

These clandestine meetings went on for nearly a year. They reminded Joe of their brief courtship, when the bazaar had been their ruse to be in each other's company.

Annette enjoyed these sneaky moments away from home. Yet, she refused to acknowledge Joe's presence in the building. When Joe sought an explanation from her, she said that she didn't want to irk Benji. Then, as an afterthought, she mentioned how she feared that her husband would kill Joe, and losing her dear friend wasn't something she could live to see. It made Joe feel good, though he didn't realise that the thought had struck her only later. Benjamin, despite being the mess he was, had always been Annette's priority.

Their platonic affair was gratifying, and Joe would not have wanted it to go any other way. Those stolen hours of conversation each day brought momentary relief to him and calmed his longing for her.

His love for Annette had never really been a physical one. What he felt for her was out of the ordinary. He could see the difference between what he shared with Rose Maria and what he had with Annette. With the former, his carnal needs were well taken care of. He was having more than his fair share of sex daily, and he would be lying if he said that he didn't enjoy it.

With Annette, he did not feel the need to cross that bridge. The fact that she never tormented him in his dark, erotic fantasies was reason enough for him to believe that his love for her had transcended the material. And maybe Rose Maria covered so much ground in that department that those desires, though lurking, did not crop up when he met Annette.

But that same year, on the night of 15 September, everything he had pieced together disappeared in the blink of an eye.

Joe was fast asleep, wrapped in the arms of Rose Maria, when a bad dream woke him up at around 2.30 a.m. With beads of sweat caking his freckled face, Joe headed to the kitchen to drink water. He was fiddling with the lid of the matka where they stored water, when he heard faint sobs from above. Bosco's wooden structure had always made it possible for neighbours to snoop into the lives of each other, but the silence of the night made it far easier for voices to travel.

This particular sound was so distinct that Joe knew immediately where it was coming from. He was closing in towards the kitchen window to find out what was going on, when the noise of a bottle crashing to the floor alarmed him. The cries got louder after that.

Without much thought, Joe Crasto walked out of his home and hurriedly climbed up the wooden stairs to ring his neighbour's doorbell. A distraught Annette opened the door.

'What are you doing here?' she asked, between sobs.

'I heard you cry. Is he beating you up again?'

'Leave now, Joe. It's just one of his crazy moods.'

'Where's he? Let me deal with him.'

'No. He's my husband, and only I will handle him,' Annette choked.

'Don't be crazy, Anna,' he reproached.

'Joe, leave now,' she repeated. 'You will get both of us killed,' she said, worried that if he stood there any longer, a storm would definitely brew.

Watching the love of his life cry made Joe feel more powerless and miserable than ever. He wanted to hold her, wrap her in his arms and protect her. Joe didn't know what came upon him then, but all at once he grabbed Annette by the waist and pulled her closer to place a long hard kiss on her lips. Despite the unexplainable joy it brought him, this had definitely not been part of the plan.

The slap that followed was not something he saw coming. Another one hit him right across the face, and now Annette was howling loudly, punching him in his chest.

'How dare you?' she asked, shocked. 'How dare you take advantage of my situation?'

Right then, she heard Benjamin approach them. 'Never, ever show that face of yours to me again. I hate you, Joe. I hate you,' she said, and without even giving Joe a moment to clarify his behaviour, she slammed the door on him.

Joe stood there for a while, cold as a zombie. Inside, he heard Annette shriek. Somebody had slapped someone, he wasn't sure who. He heard the thud of a door, the breaking of a chair and the crashing of another bottle, and then suddenly, nothing else.

When everything around him had turned silent, he walked downstairs slowly. With each step, his feet came down heavier. His eyes had welled up, but the tears did not roll down. He tried and tried, but he couldn't shed a drop. Only his eyes grew hazy and fogged his vision.

When he reached home, he could feel his body turn to stone. He forced himself to sit down on the sofa as every nerve within him shut down one heartbeat at a time. Joe had come undone, exhausted by one woman's brazen indifference to his fate. He loved, but had never been loved. He lived, but never really lived.

Before his eyes finally curled to a close, Joe yelped one last time. The sound was so agonising that it echoed through the house. It woke up Mrs Rose Maria Crasto, but the darkness revealed nothing. Not even Joe's death.

7

THE WATER FIASCO

October 2003

In this old, rickety building comprising six flats over three floors, new neighbours arrived. A family of six: a couple with three boys and a baby girl. After a decade in Dubai's arid but abundant landscape, they had shifted to Mumbai, occupying the flat on the second floor of 193-A, Bosco Mansion.

The news thrilled all the residents of Cavel, considering how swiftly its Catholic population had dwindled. The neighbourhood was overrun by enterprising Gujaratis and Marwaris, who were buying properties at dirt-cheap rates in the hope of spinning real-estate magic. But the excitement aside, nothing disturbed the occupants of Bosco more than the thought of how the municipal water would now be distributed in the houses.

The other residents, all ageing, totalled only six, with an old woman—either widowed or single—in each flat. There was the two-time widow Rose Maria, aged eighty-seven, who lived on the ground floor. The first-floor flats were occupied by sexagenarian Ellena Gomes and sixty-five-year-old Annette da Cunha. The second floor had had only one resident for a very long time, the nonagenarian Tresa Lawrence. The only married pair was the Coutinhos who, like the others, were riding into the sunset, and whose children, much to their displeasure, refused to return to India. Merlyn Coutinho's happiness knew no bounds when she learnt that a family, and a very young one at that, was moving in.

'*Kitté munta re?* Kids in our building. It will be like the good old days again, na Michael?' Merlyn told her husband, as her neighbour and the building's secretary, Ellena, who sat at the other end of the Coutinhos' drawing room, rambled about the hubbub they were to expect, now that the building was going to be home to four young children.

At five feet and seven inches, Ellena was taller than most women Michael had ever known. Her broad shoulders and oddly compartmentalised body fat made her look even bigger, while her thick-rimmed glasses, which magnified her deep-set eyes and aquiline nose, added to her intimidating personality. She usually wore loose-fitting cotton dresses in different shades of blue that covered her from head to knee, exposing her swollen feet. A car had run over her legs in an accident that crushed her bones and caused a temporary disfigurement. After years of walking with the help of crutches, she was slowly regaining strength, but any extra effort would cause her feet to swell.

Ellena was to Bosco Mansion what antique furniture was to a home. Sixty-nine, unmarried, with no family to tend to and nobody to call her own, the former librarian occupied her retirement years prying into other people's lives, mostly those of her immediate neighbours. Always privy to the gossip in Cavel thanks to Laxmi, the maid she shared with Merlyn, Ellena never gave up an opportunity to condescendingly comment about people in her parish, or even those beyond her line of vision. She had an opinion, mostly an intelligent one, about every soul who had ever lived and breathed, even the celebrities and politicians whose names showed up in the newspapers. Residents of the neighbourhood dreaded her courtesy visits to their homes. Those who refused to open the door to her often became the butt of spurious gossip. A few patronised her by agreeing with every word she said, treating her as the final authority on Dr D'Lima Street. But one couldn't take away the fact that she was the most well-informed and knowledgeable person in the area, generously parting with trivia on Cavel in some dear hope that the residents would feel the same pride she did in being associated with this quaint locality.

She knew its history down pat—one building, for instance, had seen three mayors of Bombay within thirty years; in the 1870s, Padaria de Cavel (Bakery of Cavel) that had been started by baker Salvador Patricio de Souza of Assagao, Goa, had been one of the greatest depots of bread the city had ever seen, hiring several Maharashtrian women and men to pound, knead and sweat under the glow of the fire-lit ovens and to distribute thousands of loaves of bread daily; an educational institution, set up even before the Catholic School of Cavel, was among the oldest in South Mumbai, having opened first in 1782. 'We are living on a gold mine,' she'd say.

What, however, made her unpopular was her loathing of children. She disliked them from the bottom of her resentful heart. When she wasn't staring down the kids who came to play in the compound, she was finding newer ways to get rid of them. People claimed that Ellena's cold demeanour had a lot to do with her own disciplined childhood, which involved little play and long hours invested in studies and music. She was a gifted pianist. Ellena expected children to be regimented into the rigours of academics and taught how to excel in the arts, instead of being allowed to create a racket playing hockey, football or that dangerous game of cricket, where balls as hard as stone would dramatically crash into the windows of homes.

But how much she had looked forward to playing with Michael as a child, when her father would allow her only thirty minutes of playtime on Sundays, and how she eventually ended up earning such a devilish distinction for herself were still not known. Because as weird as it sounds, Ellena had once loved everything she had now come to hate. At the top of this list was Michael.

Only Ellena knew how dear Michael had been to her. She had a few forgettable relationships in her life, one with a married man twice her age, but nothing felt real, at least compared to what she imagined would have happened with Michael. Ellena got so tired of this failed pursuit of love that she eventually decided against marrying; she couldn't think of allowing anybody else into the space she had once carved out for this man. Unfortunately, she loved Michael at a time when his mind was occupied by thoughts of Tracey. When he snapped out of it, he—to everyone's shock—married Merlyn from Khotachi Wadi. Ellena never stood a chance.

Her mother Giselle suspected that her daughter was obsessed with Michael. It could have been true then, but it was another story today. Ellena hated Michael's impertinence as much as he hated her guts. They wouldn't have made a happy couple, that much Ellena was sure of. The only thing tolerable about him now was Merlyn, his wife.

'It's been so long since we've had children here. I think almost fifteen years,' Ellena said, trying to distract the couple. 'I think the last kid at Bosco was Ryan. Good thing that he followed Sarah and went to Canada. There has been so much peace after that. Bosco feels like a great retirement home. I don't know how I am going to cope with having a family around.'

She would have continued, but Merlyn cut her short. 'What do you mean re, Ellena? My kids were bad?'

'No, no, no, no,' Ellena said nervously. 'That is not what I meant, darling. You raised such sweethearts; they still send me Christmas cards every year. They were so well-mannered and talented. But children today …' She sighed.

'Don't fall for that, Merlyn. She is humouring you. You know the tough time she gave us when Ryan was around,' Michael snickered and went back to his eveninger.

By nature, Michael was loud-mouthed, and with Ellena, more so. When he was around her, he didn't bother filtering his conversations, not realising that though she was such a tough nut, she had a heart too. Even now, as the words tumbled out of his mouth, they dropped a sour echo in Ellena's ears, bringing back painful memories.

As a ten-year-old, Ryan had once accidentally rammed into Ellena while chasing his friend during a cat-and-mouse game in their building compound. Ellena's market bags fell, and her vegetables scattered. A terrified Ryan apologised, but Ellena grabbed the teary-eyed boy by his collar and dragged him to his home to dole out advice to his father on good parenting.

She was hardly prepared for what was to come. After patiently listening to Ellena, Michael, who was struggling very hard to contain his anger as he watched her hold Ryan like a ready-to-butcher chicken, pulled his son to his side and punched the door Ellena was standing against. He also lifted his hand to slap her, but Merlyn and the kids managed to intervene. It didn't end there. Michael hurled horrid abuses that singed Ellena's nerves like hot iron on skin, and warned her against stepping into his house again. Poor Ellena stood quiet through the showdown, both horrified and hurt.

On that very day, Ellena stopped moping about unrequited love. Michael had lost his special place in her heart. Love begets love. Hate begets hate. But this hate caused Ellena to act recklessly. Or so her mother thought. Until then, Ellena had shown little interest in the men who fawned over her. At thirty-six, she had not had a single affair, and her spinsterhood became a matter of pride. She was obviously not your run-of-the-mill woman. Her beauty came from her intelligence, and she wore it on her sleeve with confidence. But suddenly, she stopped ignoring the overtures of fifty-eight-year-old Haider Ali, a history professor who visited the library where she worked and who spoke less to her and more to her breasts. What had initially repelled her suddenly seemed attractive and tempting. She had to give in before he lost interest and so, one day when he as usual claimed to have not found a book that he needed—an excuse he gave often so that she'd come with him to a secluded corner of the library, and he could get an eyeful of her breasts as she searched between books—she went with him. She undid a few buttons of her shirt and allowed him to cop a feel that day, and the next and the next. Ali was a married man, with seven children; his oldest daughter was Ellena's age. A future together seemed bleak. So when a few weeks later he suggested they spend a weekend in a hotel room, she called time on their affair.

Ellena had never been more ashamed of herself. This was never about love. It was not about lust either. It was pure hate. And it had turned her into her own enemy. From there on, she was careful with her choices. But neither of the two other romances she had, both arranged by her mum, lasted beyond a few months.

Meanwhile, Ellena's indifference made Michael more resolute. When she snubbed him at a dinner party some days after the fight, he returned the favour by not inviting her for any celebrations thereon. He even ensured that Christmas sweets from his home never went to hers; a tradition started by their parents thus came to an end. The gulf became so wide that the two wouldn't speak to each other for the next seven years or so.

It all changed after Ellena's mum took ill. When aunty Giselle was on life support, it was Michael, and not Ellena's siblings, who stayed at the hospital with her. When her mum died a few days later, he made arrangements for the funeral, leaving Ellena to grieve. The kindness warmed Ellena's heart, and she extended the olive branch by sending across cake and chips for the family. Yet, nobody apologised for the incident involving Ryan. They continued with their lives, only this time behaving as if that fight had never occurred.

'It was a case of selective amnesia,' Michael later said.

Now, having been reminded of that incident, Ellena stood up to leave, feeling upset and humiliated. It was cruel of Michael to bring it up again, yet how could he have known how much had changed for her after that silly fight?

'I need to be back home. I am expecting a few guests,' she lied.

Merlyn realised Ellena was hurt and tried to make up for her husband's snarky behaviour. 'Forget all this, Ellena. You know how he is re,' she said, as she led her neighbour to the door.

'Merlyn, I have always wondered how such a sweet woman made it into this man's life,' Ellena replied.

'He's not so bad re.'

'You give your husband too much credit.'

Merlyn mustered a smile. 'Bye, Ellena, thank you for the good news.'

'Merlyn darling, I am not sure it will be such good news once you begin to consider how the water is going to be distributed in the building. Remember they are six and we are six,' Ellena said as she stepped out, leaving Merlyn with a lot to fret about.

Having convinced the Coutinhos of their impending doom, Ellena Gomes' job became easier. She went on to spread the bad news from one neighbour to the next, leaving a pall of gloom in the already as-good-as-dead mansion.

The problem was that of water. In the burgeoning city of Mumbai, where the ratio between the hourly-increasing population and the available basic amenities was skewed and stank of poor town planning, water was scarce and had to be rationed, just like kerosene, rice and sugar.

Like most people who lived in old buildings where water was stocked not in big tanks installed on terraces, but in buckets and water drums at home, the residents of Bosco Mansion felt the crunch.

One municipal pipeline was channelled to six flats and fed water daily for around forty-five minutes, starting at 4.30 a.m. every day. In the early years, when Dr D'Lima Street wasn't so crowded, water flushed out of the taps like heavy rain. These days, with houses around the corner illegally installing booster pumps, each flat barely managed to fill five to seven buckets. Top-floor residents suffered the most. The taps choked, splayed and stilled at their own will, and the water that made its way upwards from the rust-ridden, corroded municipal pipes brought to mind a dehydrated body relieving itself. The force of the water was so abysmal during the summer months that if you turned on the taps, tiny drops would beat languidly into the hungry steel buckets creating a lazy rhythm that brought joy to no one.

A solution was found when Michael's plumber Jeevan installed pumps in all homes above the ground floor. Yet, that did not mean that water could be used to one's heart's content. Until now, a mutual understanding among the residents of the five occupied flats had ensured six buckets full for each household, with the Coutinhos bargaining for an extra bucket so they could water the plants in the garden, and Annette da Cunha, who lived above them, requesting half a bucket more because of her embarrassing diarrhoea problem that resurfaced every two days.

Until some years ago, Merlyn had needed at least three buckets for her garden. On the insistence of the residents of the building, she had got rid of most of her plants. The chiku tree had fallen down, so the problem was partly taken care of.

It was to this water-starved building that the Braganzas came to make a new home for themselves. New neighbours meant a bucket less for each home, but after so much compromise already, no one was willing to make that sacrifice. None warned the family of their imminent troubles, not even the landlord who had given them the flat, which had been vacant for over thirty-five years. When the Braganzas settled down, Ellena Gomes and their other neighbours expected a huge uproar. They were prepared for it and unwilling to budge on the earmarked water distribution.

But day one passed, and there was not a single complaint from anyone. Day two and the water arrangement continued to remain unaffected, despite the presence of the family of six. Day three: apart from the commotion created by the kids running up and down the wooden stairs—which brought great misery to Ellena—all was normal. Everyone was feeling apprehensive, but nobody dared to talk about it, scared that the Braganzas would demand a bucket or two more.

'Let us not jinx our own happiness,' the widowed Annette da Cunha told Ellena over the phone when the latter suggested that the issue be discussed in a residents' meeting.

On day four, the Coutinho couple dropped by at Ellena's house after paying a visit to the Braganzas.

'Great mannered kids,' Merlyn informed Ellena. 'Go meet them re.'

'Oh! Well. Forget that. Did they grumble about the water problem in the building? After all, they have come from Dubai. I don't think they are used to having no water,' Ellena said, her curiosity in full spate.

'Naa, nothing they said re.'

'Strange, don't you think, Merlyn?' Ellena asked. 'Do they even take a bath? I mean, were the children clean? You know, I am just checking. Anything is possible these days … all talcum powder, no soap,' she said, breaking into a laugh.

'What you saying, simply. They looked very clean re.'

'Aah! Then I need to go and check how much water they have been using.'

Michael, who was quietly observing Ellena trying to stoke a fire, interrupted. 'Come on, Ellena, spare them your grief. You need to stop behaving like an old cat. They are happy, so are we. Leave them alone, will you?' he said bluntly.

That rude remark from her arch-nemesis did not stop Ellena from prying into the lives of the Braganzas. As a daily practice, she would peek through the curtains of her balcony to see Shane Braganza leave for work in his car, followed by his wife Christabell, who'd drop her three young boys to the school bus. They all looked impeccably tidy, and it didn't look like the trick of some scented powder for sure.

Similarly, in the evenings when the boys came down to play, their mother would join them, a wet towel turbaned around her head. It meant that she was having a head bath daily. From where did she get all that water, Ellena wondered.

After a month had passed without a single complaint from the Braganzas, Ellena decided to check on the family herself. She couldn't fathom why her new neighbours hadn't raised a stink when the rest of the building had not had a good night's sleep in years over the water issue.

Christabell, who was at home with her young daughter, greeted her at the door.

'It's so lovely to see you. I've heard so much about you from everyone here,' said Christabell. She was a tall and heavy woman; her shoulders drooped from the weight of her year-old daughter whom she had strapped to her chest in a carrier.

'I hope you've heard good things, darling,' Ellena said. 'Generally, people around here hate me.'

'Well. That's not true,' Christabell lied, remembering how just the other day, Michael had warned her to keep away from that 'old cat of Bosco' when the family had gone to the Coutinhos' home for dinner.

The Braganzas' home smelled of fresh paint. There were interesting embellishments in the flat—the miracle of Gulf money, Ellena thought. The modern-day light fixtures, for instance. The huge flat-screen television. A massive leather couch. The red Persian rug. Faux-wood flooring in the drawing room, which gave the home a classy touch.

'I presume you sweep and mop your house daily?' Ellena enquired, as she made herself comfortable on a chair.

Christabell nodded, not knowing what to say. 'Should I get you some tea?'

'Oh! Don't bother with that,' Ellena said. 'I like your home. Clean and spotless,' she went on.

'Thank you, Ellena.'

That Christabell wasn't parting with any information was driving Ellena up the wall. After a brief pause and a lot of deliberation on how best to get information out of her, Ellena asked, 'Christabell darling, I hope I am not prying too much, but could you tell me how much water you use to mop the floor of your home?'

When she saw a look of amusement on the woman's face, she thought she needed to explain herself better. 'You know, my maid Laxmi uses very little water to mop the floor. And then the floor looks dirtier than before.' She didn't tell Christabell that because of the water situation, she only mopped her floor once a month.

'Oh! My maid uses two buckets, Ellena. One with plain water and another with phenyl.'

Two! The figure hit Ellena's head like a hammer. And that too for cleaning the floors while she barely got six buckets daily! What a waste! she thought to herself.

Observing the old woman break into a cold sweat, Christabell asked, 'Ellena, are you okay? You look off. Should I get you some water?'

'No, I am okay. Just a little flustered. I think my blood pressure just shot up. Can I use your bathroom, dear?'

'Yes, sure,' Christabell said and led Ellena inside.

To Ellena's shock, the faucet in the bathroom was running at full force. It was 11 a.m., and municipal water never came at this time. There was also a Western toilet. When Ellena tried using it, it sprayed what she quantified as almost half a bucket of water. She hurried out and decided to ask Christabell the source of the unlimited water in her home.

'Christabell, do you get continuous water supply?' she asked, throwing her an accusatory glance.

'No, Ellena, of course not, it's the municipal water.'

'Then how is your faucet running even now?'

Slightly taken aback, Christabell said, 'I don't understand what you mean. It's the municipal water, stored in a tank.'

'Tank! There's a tank in this building?' Ellena was shocked beyond belief.

'There is one on the roof.'

'You have a tank! When did you install it? Who gave you the permission?' Ellena asked, shaking with fury.

'Ellena, please calm down. We did not install anything. There was one when we came here.'

Unable to calm her nerves, Ellena said, 'Take me to the tank.'

Only the Braganzas and ninety-year-old Tresa Lawrence, both of whom lived on the top floor, had access to the roof. But considering Tresa's age and deteriorating health, it seemed unlikely that she'd ever consider trips to the roof unless she desired to ascend higher above, to God's home.

After struggling up the unsteady wooden ladder with Christabell carefully trailing behind her, when Ellena finally reached the flat surface of the roof, she saw what she had so badly wanted all these years: a black water tank.

As she tried to keep her balance, her eyes caught three pipelines jutting out of the tank. She went and peered down at the rear of the building. What she saw was a work of genius. While one pipeline was directed to the Braganzas, the next ended at the home of Annette, who lived right below them, and the last stopped at the Coutinho residence.

Ellena climbed down the ladder and thanked Christabell before leaving.

That evening, a note was dropped into the mailboxes of the Coutinhos. Michael had the ill-fortune of reading it first:

The secretary of Bosco Association has decided to re-work the water distribution system in Bosco Mansion. In light of the recent developments—that of the arrival of our new neighbours and a newly discovered water connection created for the convenience of a handful of residents—our previous agreement on water distribution stands nullified. Beneficiaries of this new water arrangement will now have to look for alternative sources to manage their gardens and survive bouts of diarrhoea as their old water pipelines will soon be plugged. For the record, the municipality has agreed to intervene and has promised to act on my complaint at the soonest. No meetings will be held to negotiate terms and conditions. No regret for any inconvenience caused. Regards, Ellena G.

Michael rushed to the phone. He dialled his sister's number. 'Annette! The old cat found the tank. We are busted.'

8

DEAREST BUTTERFLY, WITH LOVE

June–November 2007

Michael Coutinho,
193-A, Bosco Mansion, Flat No 1,
Dr D'Lima Street, Chira Bazaar,
Mumbai 4000002

18 June 2007

Dear Michael,
I met Patrick and Joana Misquitta from Pius House at church this morning. They are down for a short vacation in Goa; we later caught up for lunch at my home. It's been months since I met someone from Cavel. Living where I do, I am practically isolated from the rest of the world.

It's from them that I learnt about Merlyn. I am sorry, but I wasn't aware. Please accept my heartfelt condolences. Pat told me everything, and I am yet to come to terms with it myself. My loss is not as huge as yours, but it pains me to know that she is not around anymore. She was the life and soul of Bosco Mansion, and I can't even imagine that place without her. A deep sadness fills me, but I want to speak little of it as it comes at the cost of compounding your own grief.

I know this letter of mine may take you by surprise since we haven't spoken in four years. But this tragedy is too huge for us to hold grudges. Let's just forget and forgive. What happened, happened in the past, and I'd appreciate a fresh start. Give my regards to Ryan and Sarah when you speak with them next. Tell them I miss their mother too.

Warm regards,
Ellena G.

— —

Ellena Gomes,
Casa Gomes, SocoilloWaddo,
Pernem, Goa

29 June 2007

Dear Ellena G.,
Your last letter was very vague. Do you mean that we are back to being friends again? If so, then there is so much to tell you. And since I don't want to waste time waiting for your response, I am going with my gut and writing to you as only an old friend would.

To begin with, thank you for your letter. It's very kind of you to have written. I really do miss Merlyn every single second of the minute of the hour of the day. She was my life and soul as much as she was Bosco's. But it has been two months, and I know I cannot continue like the living dead.

Sarah and Ryan suggested that I join them in Montreal. But I absolutely hate the winters there. People get so excited about white Christmases. I used to be that way too. But nobody tells you how lonely it can get. Also, to be honest, I would rather die alone in the home that Merlyn and I built together than on foreign soil. The kids eventually gave up and left last month, though I must mention that they didn't try too hard.

They always had Merlyn to take their side. I doubt they'd find a good replacement in me. The idea of kids moving too far away from parents has always discomfited me. I know that's life and all, but still. Imagine if I had abandoned them when they were younger.

You do remember that time when I had a chance to take up an offer at a newspaper in London? It's another thing that the role was of a junior staff reporter when I had fifteen years of experience on my side. I should have gone anyway. It was London. But I didn't because of mama. Dad died too soon. How could I leave her alone with Annette and her drunk better half?

Do children think that way anymore? I tell you all this knowing very well how much you loved and adored your own mother. You stayed with aunty Giselle right till the end, when your six and counting family escaped to the States and Canada. Need I say, I respected you for that. Sorry, I am whining. I will end this letter right here, right now.

Regards,
Michael

P.S. Amused at how you insist on keeping the first letter of your surname even now. Old habits die hard. Don't they?

——

5 July 2007

Dear Michael,

I wasn't vague. We have always been friends, but of course, there have been rough days. I think they have finally passed. It was so nice hearing from you. I was drying clothes on the lawn when our postman, Roy D'Costa, came around with your letter. He said, 'Do people still write letters?' I gave him an encouraging smile.

Then I left everything I was doing and read your letter. Nobody writes to me, especially none of my 'six and counting' family. So you can imagine my excitement on hearing from you.

My mother always told me that having a family around was important. She believed that they were the only ones who stuck with you through thick and thin. I wasn't lucky in that department. When mother died, my brothers said that they were too old to even manage a walk in their own lawns, let alone fly down for the funeral. I knew it was too much for them to spend on flight tickets, so I kept quiet. How would I have even managed without you and Merlyn? But I am sure your children are trying. At least they come and visit you once in a while. Consider yourself in a better place.

How do you spend your time now? I can proudly say that I am improving. I now find kids tolerable. I teach my maid Lorna's young girls for two hours in the afternoon. Yesterday, we read Jane Austen. But I think they prefer Ruskin Bond. So I am reading Bond these days, but he writes a lot about ghosts. The maid doesn't charge me for her work, and I don't charge her for mine. It works well for both of us.

Regards,
Ellena

P.S. Note: The G has vanished.

—

15 July 2007

Dear Michael,
No news from you yet. Did I offend you with my uncalled-for advice? Did I whine too much? Forgive this lonely woman. It's hard to be good.

Regards,
Ellena

P.S. Note, the G has 'really' vanished.

—

4 August 2007

Dear Ellena,
Your letters are funny. You helped me sail through the last month. I read and re-read them to feel better. It was Merlyn's birthday on 10 July, and try as I did, I could

not bring myself to do anything. She would have turned seventy-two. I was actually doing fine that day. I woke up, had tea with bun-maska and sat to read the newspaper, following it up with your letter, which had been sitting on my table from the day before. Then Sarah called from Montreal. She said, 'Dada, mom was still too young to die. Don't you think?'

I knew in my heart of hearts that Sarah was right. If only I had not taken her mild headaches lightly, I could have saved her. After that, I just lost the will to do anything till I sat down to write this letter today.

Can you imagine a life filled with anxious days and sleepless nights? Well, that's how I spend my time. She was not too old. Was she?

I am glad you are becoming a better person, Ellena. And you know this is not personal. I always thought there was hope for you! It's just that you were too tough for your own good. That never made you a bad person; it just made you a terrible human being. Okay, jokes apart, I still admired you.

The caterpillar is evolving. Getting rid of the letter 'G' is a good start. Be more affectionate to the kids; they will love you more than any of your 'six and counting' family ever could.

Regards,
Me, Mike

P.S. Note: Caterpillar still has the old 'cat' hiding within. When will you turn into a butterfly?

— —

15 September 2007

Dear Michael,

What was so funny about my letters? Is it the fact that a terrible human being is trying to turn over a new leaf? You haven't changed, have you? Honestly, your last letter left me fuming. I had half a mind not to reply to you. And I was doing quite well. I also burnt the letter, so that I never had to read it again. Then yesterday, you called on my landline. I heard the 'hello' and instantly knew it was you. I was still angry and did not want to speak, so I thought I would write and clear up the differences instead.

Mind you, I am still angry. I am only forgiving you because Merlyn is not around. I don't want a lonely man to feel lonelier. And clearly, your children aren't helping either. Spend your time doing better things, Michael. Stop being so snarky all the time. Go to church and talk to God instead of wallowing in your sorrows. It helps.

Regards,
Ellena G.

P.S. People like you cut my wings every time I try to fly. How can I ever turn into a butterfly?

— —

20 September 2007

Dear Ellena,

You are a strange woman. You take offence at everything. I really don't know what to filter anymore. When I said you were funny, I was referring to your postscripts. You are free to not believe me, but I am anyway attaching copies of your letters so that you re-read them to know what I am talking about. Since you have burnt my previous letter, I am sending a copy of that too. Please go back to it and highlight what part seemed offensive and 'snarky'. We can discuss it in the next letter.

As a habit, I always keep an extra copy of what I write for myself. Merlyn always found it funny. If she were alive, she would finally know why I did it. I am, however, glad you forgave me. I don't think I can wait for another tragedy before we start talking again. The only tragedies waiting to happen now are our own funerals. Let us not push it.

Regards,
Michael

P.S. I see that the 'G' has re-appeared. Looks like the 'cat'erpillar will have to wait before it tries to fly again. Also, I did not call you. It's scary to know that there are people who sound just like me. Merlyn loved my voice. She said it was one of a kind. Thank God, she never heard this man. I wouldn't rule out adultery. See what he made you do. You are writing to me again. I had also mentioned that your letters helped me sail through my worst moments, but you ignored that completely.

— —

30 September 2007

Dear Ellena,
I reiterate, 'you are a strange woman'. You only sent me a copy of my letter with highlighted portions without

mentioning what really irked you. What explanation do you want? Okay, I agree I called you terrible, but that was meant to be a joke. If it hurt you, I apologise. In your words, I don't want a lonely woman to feel any lonelier. Also, why exactly have you highlighted the cat in caterpillar, when I already put it in single quotes for you? I have called you that for decades. Do you want me to call you something else? Like, say, 'Butterfly'? Would that get you to talk to me again?

I was, however, most amused with your efficiency in tracing the phone-call details from the state telephone company. Yes, it was me on the other end. I presumed that you were not happy with my last letter, and so I called. Can't this old man play tricks? Also, I am not a fan of the silent treatment.

Regards,
Me, Mike

P.S. Fly, fly, fly. I lost my scissors; I can't cut your wings, pretty little butterfly.

— —

4 October 2007

Dear Mike,
Wasn't that what I called you when we were kids? I still remember. Now that we are done talking business, I feel much better and less slighted.

My postman Roy is pleased that I use his services. Nobody in the area uses him for real letters anymore, only drafts and money orders.

He knows very little English, and only speaks Konkani. Oh, how I miss Merlyn on these occasions. She was excellent at it. You know how bad my Konkani is, right? Roy and I struggle to communicate, yet I enjoy meeting him. He comes by to have tea in the mornings (sometimes with your letters) and teaches me some simple Konkani words. I tutor him in English. He thinks I have a lover in Bombay. It's hard to convince people, so I told him that you call me an old cat and think I am terrible with people. Now he tells me that I am writing to a horrible person and fighting for a good word when I am already such a wonderful human being. I like this concocted story. We should keep it that way.

Regards,
Elle

P.S. That's what Mike called me.

— —

11 October 2007

Dearest Butterfly,
Congratulations, you finally have wings. Dainty, petite, and colourful, like the Elle from many years ago. You are hobnobbing with kind people. You should have let him believe that we are lovers. Why make me such a horrible man? On your advice, I go to church every morning. Then I go to the fish market and buy something new. Today, we made jhinga masala fry. I also asked the maid to make me some prawn balchão

so I can have it with pao for breakfast. Remember your mum made it during the monsoon? She'd always keep an extra bottle for me.

Laxmi grumbles, but she makes it anyway. She feels sorry for me. I don't mind this sympathy because I get my way. Christabell's daughter, Sharon, comes down to the compound in the evenings, and I teach her to cycle. Things are getting better here. Also, I don't speak to the kids these days. When they call, I get Laxmi to talk to them. I won't have them rub salt into my wounds when they walked out of our lives nearly twenty years ago. Annette comes in the evening for tea. Do you realise we never spoke of her even once in our letters? The good news is that she has been bearable of late. Or maybe she is feeling sorry for me too. At least tea times go without an argument.

Now that we are back to being friends, I think it is time I clear up the issues we had regarding the water pipeline. Remember when you were in Goa for a year after that accident? We got the municipality to sanction us a pipeline then. According to the civic rules, we were eligible for another line to our building. Nothing was illegal. I am sorry we hid it from you. It was completely Annette's and my idea. For once, she and I were on the same page. But to be fair to the rest of the neighbours, we never filled the seven buckets of water that we said we did. We just took three buckets that Merlyn used for her garden. It was still wrong on our part, and I am sorry for that.

I see you don't ask about Cavel. Are you cheating on me? Is someone else feeding you with gossip on the town, or is the butterfly soaring towards the sky?

With love,
Mike

P.S. Try writing to me in Konkani the next time.

–––

15 October 2007

Dear Mike,

I am not cheating on you. I don't need to know anything more now that the man who is teaching me to fly is around. I am in the sky, and the view is stunning from up here. Thanks to you.

Can I be honest? Your letters make me happy. This is all I look forward to now. Does that worry you?

My Konkani is bad; Roy gave up in two days. He is picking up English quite well though. I am glad to know Annette and you are getting along. The building must be restful now. It's a nice time to live in Bosco. I was thinking of coming to Bombay next month. I need to air my house too. It has been years. Do you think it's a nice idea?

Yours,
Butterfly

P.S. Roy is back to assuming that we are lovers. Don't ask me how! Also, the pipeline issue—consider it forgotten. My memory isn't helping either.

–––

20 October 2007

Dear Ellena,

Yes, there's a nervous calm in Bosco Mansion. I doubt it has anything to do with Annette and me not fighting anymore. It's Merlyn. The building is missing her as much as I do. And you gave up on learning Konkani too soon. Bad learner you've become. What happened to the St Anne's School topper of 1949?

Regards,
Michael

— —

30 October 2007

Dear Ellena,

I like how you use my own tricks on me. I received a copy of your letter of 15 October, highlighting what I hadn't answered in my last mail. I don't think I was in the right frame of mind to respond to your questions. I was probably missing Merlyn too much. But it is only fair that you have your answers.

No, it doesn't worry me that you, of all the people I have known, look forward to my letters. It is a privilege earned only by a few. But I am not sure whether it is right to make it the 'only' thing you look forward to now, especially at this point in your life. What about your tea sessions with Roy and classes with your maid's kids? You are being too kind to an undeserving man. About coming to Mumbai, you definitely must visit. Annette is looking forward to meeting you. She will be happy to have company that suits her taste. She calls me a compromise that she made for the lack of friends in her life. Can you believe it? I need to go and buy some fish. Laxmi has promised to make bangda curry. Goodbye for now.

Regards,
Michael

—

30 November 2007

Michael,

Many years ago, way before you were married, I asked my mother if it was fine to fall in love. She said, 'Yes, of course. One must never give up on an opportunity to trip, fall and break a leg in love.' Then, as a rider, she added, 'Though, make sure that the one you lose your heart to isn't indifferent to your fall.'

Incidentally, that very same evening, you and I were climbing up the stairs to head to our respective homes after a game of badminton when I sprained my ankle. I was in deep pain, but you didn't reach out to help me. Instead, you stood there helplessly for a while, before rushing to call my mother. My mother came right away. It was she who held me in her arms, lifted me and took me back home. You didn't even bother to come along. You were probably in your room, lying on your bed, sore after that game. But so smitten was I that I foolishly believed you would come over afterwards and check on me. You didn't.

The next evening, you were already in the compound, playing badminton with Annette. You had forgotten all about me, and so conveniently.

The timing of that incident was purely coincidental, but I took it as a sign to stop pining for you. Five years later, you got married to Merlyn. Thank God for that fall on the stairs, I learned to cope with heartbreak.

When I read your letter last month, a similar feeling came to me. Was it plain indifference on your part, or was it an innocent oversight? Unfortunately, I know the answer. Only this time, I don't know whether to feel bad for myself or stupid for having allowed this to happen to me again. Michael, you have none of the charms that once caught my attention. But there—I just fell for you again.

I am returning the originals of all the letters you sent me. I don't have the copies (yes, I burned them) and neither do I need them. Do not re-send them or reply to this letter. It's time you got back to missing Merlyn.

Warm regards,
Ellena G.

P.S. Do you know that the average life of a butterfly is approximately one month? I didn't. I learned it the hard way.

9

KING OF THE CROSSWORD

May 1987

Many would call him manic, others a man possessed, but Mario Lawrence, who turned fifty in the April of 1987, did what he did only because he enjoyed solving a good crossword puzzle. If that earned him a poor reputation in Cavel, he'd say, 'so be it'.

In all these years, Mario had never had a job or drawn a salary. For a man with intelligence so exceptional, many in the township, including Michael Coutinho, considered this a pity. He did, however, manage to make at least two hundred and fifty rupees a month—it was the token prize money he received from hours of poring over riddles to fill empty square grids in newspapers. There were months when he also made an extra thirty or fifty rupees when he had solved more than his usual quota of crosswords.

Such days, however, were few and far between and didn't change anything for him or his mother, Tresa, because everything Mario ever won was invested back into honing his game. This included buying more newspapers and books that, while heavy on the pocket, helped him pack enough ammo to become the best crossword player in the city. To achieve this, Mario followed a disciplined routine.

Every morning around 7 a.m., after the paperwallah had left a pile of twenty newspapers—four copies each of three broadsheets and two tabloids—at Tresa Lawrence's home in Bosco Mansion, Mario would collect the stack from the doorstep and leave for the dingy room in the centuries-old Hari Om Niwas building, which was situated along the main road of Chira Bazaar. 'Mario saab, aaj kitna puzzle solve karega,' the paanwallah at the entrance of the building would ask on seeing him.

Mario detested small talk; he would just smile and climb the flight of stairs quietly.

Until the mid-seventies, this room had been the liveliest den in town. Tresa aunty cho add'do, as it was infamously known, on the first floor of the four-storeyed, dilapidated structure, was the place where young men from the area were first initiated into the wasting joys of drinking everything from hooch to country to port wines from Goa and home-made experiments.

When Prohibition was finally abolished in 1972, the add'do, as predicted, failed to draw revellers. After years of failed attempts to tighten the noose around the sale of booze, the Maharashtra government softened its stand and introduced a permit system that allowed each person to consume a fixed amount of alcohol. The average Joe was allowed a few pints of whisky and a dozen-odd bottles of beer per month for an annual permit of one rupee and sixty-five paise. While the excitement of drinking clandestinely could never match the kind of intoxication that had the approval of the authorities, people chose the latter as it was both convenient and legal.

Despite falling on hard times, Tresa managed the business for another four years, sustaining it on her bangda and jhinga masala fry and smooth wines, one of which was a potent cocktail of grape, orange, pineapple and ginger. It's true that she had had plans to shut down the drinking den long before Prohibition was lifted. And had her son Mario followed the script she had written for him, the taint of running this add'do would have been replaced by something more phenomenal and historic.

A year after his father, David Lawrence, died, Mario had been sent to a boarding school in Panchgani, a hill station not very far from the city, where kids of the rich and famous, especially British officers, studied. Tresa enrolled her son with the fat compensation money she had received from the shipping company following her husband's death—his body had never really come home. The intent was to keep Mario away from the gruelling life of the city and the tormenting memories of his father. She assumed that the steady pension she got each month from the Bombay Fire Brigade would help cover the exorbitant school fees. Far from it. She was soon drowning in debt. When nothing worked, Nancy, her friend from Goa who now lived in Mazagaon, introduced her to Natraja Mudaliar of Sion Koliwada.

The moment the shrewd yet affable Natraja met Tresa, he knew she'd leave no stone unturned to do this job right. He offered her a large sum of money to sell the hooch liquor that he was brewing at his distillery.

Aware that her stuck-up neighbours, who considered themselves nonpareil in Bombay's Catholic community, would not entertain her damaging enterprise, a desperate Tresa rented a tiny space a stone's throw from Cavel and made it the base for her liquor haven. There were several road-blocks, but her presence of mind helped her avoid them.

On Natraja's suggestion, she collected her hooch in a rubber tyre tube that she'd strap around her waist and shield under a flowing, umbrella dress to pull off the pregnant look. She managed it well until one day, Rajesh Pyaare, the driver of the BEST bus that she took for her trips between Wadala— where Natraja's man sold her the supply—and Chira Bazaar, noticed that she had been pregnant for over eighteen months. When he confronted her, Tresa bribed him with free drinks at her den. Some time after that, Rajesh asked her to enlist the help of his cop friend, who would dress in plain clothes and accompany her to Bombay Central, forewarning her of any bandobast ahead. He was rewarded with a monthly hafta of two rupees. Soon, Tresa developed a tight network of cops and informants who worked with and for her.

In Chira Bazaar, she earned the moniker of Chikni aunty; her pretty face gave her this distinction. Most men from Cavel, though, continued to address her only as Tresa aunty, scared that their wives would take offence.

Twelve years into the business, when Mario was at Sir JJ School of Arts, Tresa finally bought the room for a few thousand rupees from the profits she had accrued. She had done so assuming that her son, who was studying to become a sculptor, would most likely need a space to work. Her plan was to shut shop as soon as he graduated. Mario was aware of the ridicule his mum had suffered, but he never held it against her and also promised her a way out of it soon.

'This will end, mama. I promise,' he told her.

Indeed, Mario had turned into a fine, handsome man, very much in the likeness of his father. Despite hanging around with the rich brats from school, many of whom were his close friends, he never dared to smoke or take a fancy to the bottle. Instead, he invested all his free time engaging in the arts. Apart from sketching, he also had the rare talent of transforming a canvas with his bare hands. Where most people used a brush, he painted with his fingers, achieving the same, if not better, finesse in his strokes. After bagging several awards in high school for his drawings, he won a scholarship to JJ, which stood grandly opposite the regal Gothic-style station, Victoria Terminus and returned to Bombay, where Tresa had foreseen a bright career for him.

Despite shielding Mario from hardship, Tresa couldn't prevent the fate that awaited the young man, when he befriended Ranjana Banerjee, the girl he would lose his heart and mind to.

When the gorgeous Ranjana met Mario in college, her agenda was clear—she wanted a new Marxist disciple to fuel her Communist cause. Mario's shy and sensitive spirit quickly warmed to the literature she was espousing. By the time they were in the final year, love happened, and their politically charged sculpting sessions quickly extended into passionate nights of revelry in the Colaba home where she lived, with her grandmum's visually challenged sister. The old lady was oblivious to the affair, as the sharpness of her mind had been obstructed by her lack of sight.

'You should come and meet my mama,' Mario told Ranjana one night while they were in bed. 'You know, she fooled the cops all her life,' he sniggered.

'Really! How?' Ranjana asked, taking a sip of the brandy she had poured for herself. She placed the glass to Mario's lips, but he pushed it aside. 'I don't drink. How many times have I told you, Ranji?'

'Arre ... just one sip.'

'No, please.' His irritation showed.

'Achcha, forget that. You were telling me how your mother fooled the cops,' she said, placing the glass on his chest, the soft hair on his skin twirling in loops around it.

'For that you have to come home. I know you will love her. By the way, did I tell you she makes the best wine in the world?'

'You don't drink, how would you know?' she mocked.

'Ranji, my house is like a wine cellar. It certainly smells like one,' he said. 'I can tell you when the fermenting has gone bad, and when it hasn't. I know the difference just from that smell.'

'No wonder you don't drink. You are tired of breathing it daily.'

They laughed together; the sudden movement of his chest caused the drink to spill all over Mario's skin, stinging him slightly. 'I am not wasting any of that alcohol,' Ranjana said, her warm tongue already gliding through the wiry strands of hair on his chest. They went back to making love, this time more passionately.

But Ranjana had a past that was also very much her present. She had kept Mario in the dark about having being married as a child to a man thirteen years older than her. The bespectacled and righteous Sreejit Banerjee, who lived in

Durgapur, had been an ardent supporter of women's rights. When Ranjana had expressed her interest to study in Bombay, he had encouraged her to follow her dreams, provided she returned home after graduating to start a family with him. She was ashamed of how easily she had let her fluttering heart blind her to the reality that waited back home—the one that she owed this new life to.

Torn between her lover and her husband, Ranjana was forced to make a choice before things got serious. She dropped out of college barely two months before the finals, leaving the city forever. Mario never knew. He spent several days wandering about in Colaba, only to later learn from Ranjana's grand-aunt that she had moved lock, stock and barrel to her hometown and settled down with her husband of ten years.

Many years ago, when Mario was still a child, Dr Ralph McGowan, the Anglo-Indian doctor from Chira Bazaar, had urged his parents to 'shield his nerves'. Tresa had never not taken those warnings seriously. Mario, after all, was the centre of her universe, and he wasn't just any ordinary centre. He was the fulcrum of her existence, the only reason why she had chosen to live when dying had seemed so much easier.

But in Mario's life, there had been two centres—his art and his heart—and both of them were so close to each other that he possibly mistook them as being one significant whole. And so, when he lost one, he lost everything, including his universe.

For weeks on end after Ranjana left, Mario didn't come out of his bedroom, and when he finally did, he announced that he was leaving college. A week later, he stopped speaking. On Michael's insistence, Tresa took him to a psychiatrist at Masina Hospital in Byculla. His poor state—the doctor termed it a nervous shock—called for immediate admission. Tresa had never known of Ranjana and wasn't able to comprehend what exactly had gone wrong with her son.

Call it the convenience of memory, but when Mario recovered four weeks later, he could not remember anything about the woman he had loved. But the wound was so grave that at the age of twenty-two, he was no longer the same spirited young man who had returned to Bombay to pursue a career in the arts. With Ranjana's sudden exit, he lost two centres, and without them, the geometry of his life was completely awry. He forgot how to make magic with his fingers.

Thirty years on, Mario was a different person. He invested his intelligence in solving puzzles and crosswords. At 7.15 a.m. sharp, he would unlock the door of his room at Hari Om Nivas and switch on the tiny bulb that hung tenaciously from the ceiling right below the fan. There was only one small window in the tiffin-box-like space, and the sunlight that peered through the iron grille painted the room in just enough light to see the objects that occupied it. The wall adjacent to the door was stacked with dust-layered books, many of which were dictionaries and thesauruses. Think of the best names in the industry, and you'd find the hardbound copies here—Collins, Oxford, Cambridge, Merriam-Webster, Longman, Macmillan. Even the recently published American edition of Reader's Digest's *Success With Words* had made its way into Mario's collection. Right next to these books was another haphazard pile of crossword guides—Mario's most treasured possession among these was the 1949 edition of *The Complete Crossword Reference Book*, which he had purchased from Suleman Botawala, owner of

Smoker's Corner, one of the most unassuming bookstores in the city.

Suleman had started his passion project in 1953 in the foyer of the family-owned Botawala Chambers on Sir Pherozeshah Mehta Road, Fort. Soon, the store became the haunt of bibliophiles looking for rare, unusual reads. The most purchased were the DC and Dell comics, American and British magazines, the romances of Mills & Boon and popular pulp fiction, with James Hadley Chase and Surender Mohan Pathak's books topping the list.

Mario, who went about the city as and where his feet took him, first read about Smoker's Corner in the *Illustrated Weekly* magazine in the late seventies. As soon as he went there, he struck up an unlikely friendship with Suleman.

The latter was senior to him by a decade or more, but their shared interest in books made the age gap irrelevant. Mario would visit the store every Saturday afternoon, and the two would enjoy endless chats on the edge of the lofty spiral staircase inside the building over a cup of cutting chai, before discussing the new books that Suleman had procured for the store. Mario was also a patron of Smoker's Corner's lending library, where one could borrow books for as minimal a fee as three rupees.

'Don't even pay a paisa. Saab won't like it,' Suleman's staffer told Mario when he tried paying upfront. 'You are Suleman saab's dost first, customer baad mein.'

If the books in his room were a gift of the benevolence of his friend at Smoker's Corner, the several empty whisky bottles that were strewn around were the vestiges of Tresa's past. It had been over ten years since she shut shop. When

Mario started using the room for reading and his puzzle-solving pastime, Tresa asked him to give all the bottles to the raddiwallah.

'You take extra money from bottles, baba. Buy books,' she said. One would think that Mario was too lazy to dump them, or never really cared. But the bottles had stories written all over them, some of which read like his own. After Mario had recovered from his illness, he decided to help his mum for want of anything better to do. He sat in the den most evenings, relishing the banter of the drunk, whiny men. Heartbreak. Unemployment. Debts. The list of problems was endless. Listening to them helped keep away the dark cloud that hovered above him and threatened to burst inside his head.

Mario was a fighter. He was aware of his manic-depressive cycles that, among the happy highs and loathful lows, often drove him to the edge and made him feel suicidal. But he had a mother to take care of, so he struggled. He had never taken to drinking, and now avoided it more ferociously, because his doctors had told him it could aggravate his condition. Comfort, however, came from watching others intoxicate themselves. These broken objects of memory now reminded him of the people who had once been broken like him.

As soon as Mario entered the room, he would dump the papers on the table, pull over the unsteady wooden stool from the corner and, chewing on the tip of his pen, begin wracking his brain. Every two hours, Ramesh chaiwallah would quietly walk in, place a glass of cutting chai on the table and hurry off. Of late, cryptic crosswords had become quite popular among word-puzzle enthusiasts. Cryptics were tricky because each clue was a puzzle in itself. The cryptic clue, in fact, was just an attempt at misguiding you, because it didn't ever lead you directly to the solution.

'You have to solve the cryptic clue first to find the clue,' Mario once explained to Michael.

Once you finished the puzzle, you were also expected to coin a 'cryptic clue' for a word that was suggested in the crossword. Mario had a reserve of cryptic clues and so was always a step ahead of the game.

It was an isolating hobby, this puzzle. And a vexing one too. The unusual map of white and black squares that owed its symmetry only to words stared at you almost mockingly, teasing you while you struggled and strained your brain for that right combination of letters to fill the grid. It was created to challenge the brain. One gone. Fifty-nine more to go. Horizontal. Vertical. Criss-cross. Even one empty square could pull your entire game down.

When he successfully finished a crossword, Mario would fill the same answers in the other three copies of the newspaper he purchased. The cycle would be repeated with the other newspapers as well. By two in the afternoon, or sometimes even before that, his first task was done. He'd then go to the post office and mail multiple entries, marking them from the addresses of the residents at Bosco or Lobo Mansions. Most newspapers decided the winner based on lots, so it made sense to send as many entries as possible. The Coutinhos, Ellena Gomes, Rose Maria and Annette da Cunha were in the know about Mario's obsession, and were happy to oblige. If and when their names popped up in the winners' list, which was very often, Mario would collect the prize money on their behalf. When he won a little extra, he would buy a packet of mava cake from the Irani bakery, Kyani & Co., for his neighbours. 'You are lucky for me again,' he'd inform them.

Sometime during the second week of May 1987, Merlyn Coutinho received a mail from a city tabloid, *Bombay Beats*, where Mario had sent many an entry in her name. The letter read:

Dear Mrs Merlyn Coutinho,

We have noticed that you are a regular contributor to our crossword section. Your knack with cryptics and the jumbo crosswords has left all of us in the editorial department impressed. If you are keen and currently unoccupied on the job front, we'd like to discuss a business proposition that we think would benefit both you and our newspaper. Irrespective, our editor, Naresh Swaminathan Raman, is keen on meeting you on the 25th of this month, at 4 p.m. at our Tardeo office. We look forward to seeing you.

Regards,
Rita Rodrigues,
Secretary to Mr Naresh Swaminathan Raman,
Editor, *Bombay Beats*

Merlyn showed the letter to her husband when he came home later that night after a long day at work. Michael had a few more years to go before retirement, and had been recently promoted to news editor. His tasks now oscillated between thinking of fresh story ideas and delegating them to the reporters, and writing daily editorials.

When he read the letter, his lips curved in a thin smile. Why hadn't he bothered to promote Mario's talent like this, he thought to himself? Naresh had been an acquaintance during Michael's early years at *The Express*. Like him, Naresh covered politics, though for *The Free Press*. When they met at press briefings or events, they'd always chat.

'Naresh is quite a gentleman,' he told his wife. 'My gut says this is going to be good for Mario,' he added, sensing an opportunity here.

The next morning, Michael rang up Naresh to tell him of the real genius behind the crosswords. After Naresh heard the entire story, he was even more impressed. 'What are you saying, Michael? Bring this man to me now,' he said.

It took some effort and cajoling, but Michael managed to drag Mario to *Bombay Beats* that very evening.

The newsroom was a delight to observe. The clickety-clack of noisy typewriters, created by the speedy punching and lifting of keys, gave the office a rhythm of its own. A couple of scribes, mostly uppity sub-editors who were yet to get their daily stream of copy to edit, circled around a table and were engrossed in a heated debate.

Apart from a few scattered words, Michael and Mario, who were waiting outside Naresh's office, couldn't make head or tail of the conversation.

'Armchair journalism,' Michael said wistfully. 'This happens in the newsroom all the time. Just give these subs a stage, and they think they can change the world with their opinions,' he added, as if he was duty-bound to explain the strange ways of his ilk.

Mario smirked, unsure whether his opinion on the subject would even count. He had never worked in an office and wasn't sure if he was cut out for it. The only time he had held a real job was when he used to give maths and science tuition to Michael's children Sarah and Ryan. They were both adults now, and working professionals like their father. Ryan already had his migration documents in place; he was moving to Canada very soon. His sister had only recently moved there, after marriage.

'Mike, what do you think he has in mind?' Mario asked after a long silence.

'Well, he didn't tell me either.'

'If it's a job or something, you already know my views.'

'I am not going to push you into anything, Mario, and you know that. But we should at least know what this business proposition is about. If you aren't comfortable, you can always say no.'

'Hmm …'

Naresh was a pleasant-looking, amiable man from Madras. He may have been very scholarly, and his political pieces always reflected that, but he was also easy-going, drawn mostly to the ideas of youngsters, and understood the pulse of Bombay like nobody else. It made him the perfect candidate to lead a tabloid.

Michael and he were meeting after many years, but he didn't look very different from the last time they had met. The only thing heavy about his tall and lean frame was his beige suit, which immediately made him look like a man of position. Michael was almost embarrassed to sit down for fear that the bulk of his belly would show.

When Michael commented about how fit he looked, Naresh joked, 'Arre yaar, we are idli-sambar people. Never ate an animal in our life. Where is the scope for fat?'

The joviality continued, making the meeting seem less formal.

The offer was simple: 'We want indigenous crosswords.'

Two years after its launch in 1979, *Bombay Beats* was the only paper in the city to offer giant crosswords, which were clear winners among readers. The crossword supply came from an award-winning crossword-maker in London, whose services were also enlisted by several newspapers abroad.

'But we are a Bombay paper, yaar, and we need local flavour to win more fans like you,' Naresh told Mario. 'I want Sridevi, Shiv Sena and vada pav in my crossword. I need someone to dig out names of things, places and people from the gullies of Bombay and fit them into these square grids. It should be about our culture, people and food, yaar, not about the Big Ben and the Queen or that English breakfast. Forty years since Independence, and we are still not decolonised. You know what I mean?' He spoke on the subject with the same passion that Mario had for playing the game.

When he had finished with his over-enthusiastic spiel, Naresh said, 'I think you can make these puzzles. You have it in you, Mario.' He offered Mario an upfront salary of two thousand five hundred rupees. It wasn't a paltry sum for generating one crossword puzzle five days a week.

But while the offer was great, Mario had his doubts, and there were many.

'Mr Raman, I have never made a crossword before. I am a crossword solver, not a creator,' he said.

'Correct me if I am wrong, but haven't you studied it to the tee?' Naresh asked.

'Yes, maybe.'

'Then why do you doubt yourself, mister?' Naresh asked.

'Can I be honest, Mr Raman? I am not cut out for an office set up. And at fifty, it feels like a late start for me,' Mario said earnestly, hoping that Naresh would change his mind.

'Better late than never, boy,' Naresh said. 'And wait, you are fifty? You look like you're in the late-thirties. Tell me, do you have kids?'

'No,' Mario replied hesitantly. He wanted to mention that he wasn't married either, but held back.

'Aah, no wonder. Do you see these grey strands on my head? They are a gift from my teenage son,' Naresh joked. Mario chuckled. The ice had thawed.

Tresa Lawrence could barely contain herself when Michael broke the news to her. At seventy-five, she had settled for happiness in the little things—like when her son helped her make wine, now distributed to wedding caterers, or when they'd go to his favourite garden in the evenings so she could exercise her muscles, or the last time, five years ago, when they went to Goa together. While she had once wished he had a job, and that he was married and had children, she had resigned to this fate as her own doing.

'You saying, my baba got job?' she asked Michael again, to be doubly sure.

'Yes, aunty, and now he is going to work in a newspaper like me.'

'But it is safe, no?' she enquired. 'No goonda will be after him?' Tresa remembered an incident from five years ago when Michael had written about the rise of underworld goons from Bhendi Bazaar, and how they had all the politicians in their pockets. A few days later, the same goons came looking for

Michael at Bosco Mansion and threatened all the residents with dire consequences if they did not turn him in. But none of them gave in. They said he had moved out a long time ago.

Michael had been holidaying with his family in Goa then, and had been unaware of what happened. When they returned, he sought police protection, which he was granted for a while. To save himself more trouble, he grew a beard, and the disguise served him well. It was only a matter of time before he became too fond of his facial hair and refused to let go of it.

'No, no, aunty, don't worry. Mario is not writing about the mafia. He is only going to make crosswords.'

On 20 May, instead of going into his dungeon at Hari Om Niwas, Mario left for work at 8.30 a.m. sharp. Tresa had woken up early that day and walked all the way to Cross Maidan, nearly a kilometre from home, to light a candle at the cross that came to the aid of many in their hour of need. She returned home right on time to pack her son the dabba his father had been most fond of: dal—she called it dol—and rice with dried bombil pickle.

Excited as she was, she couldn't believe that after all these years, her son, like many other men his age, would have a nine-to-five job. She had aged quickly after downing the shutters on her add'do and withered further when her son developed an unhealthy obsession for solving puzzles. Now, if only Mario would settle down and give her a grandchild soon, she'd be able to go to heaven and show her husband her face. Wishful thinking, after all, felt like the order of the day.

Mario had found his raison d'être. He had initially requested a few weeks of preparation before the crosswords went live. Once he was ready and Naresh, a cross-enthusiast himself, was satisfied with the product Mario had created, the order came: 'Let's go to print.'

In the span of a few months, the 'Bombay Jumbo Crossword by Mario Lawrence' became a super hit. Mario's perspicacity with word puzzles and his own interest in the history of the city made his job effortless. On average, the tabloid received over one hundred and fifty entries. And despite balancing two tasks—that of creating the crosswords and sifting three winners daily—Mario remained imperturbable.

Tresa was basking in his success. As she walked through D'Lima Street, her market bags in hand, she could hear everyone say aloud, 'Chikni aunty's son is now the King of Crosswords.'

10

LETTING GO

February 1976

Benjamin da Cunha had to die. He was plain evil. The man had the same effect on the Coutinho family as Amjad Khan's character Gabbar Singh had on the villagers of Ramgarh in *Sholay*. Michael Coutinho had watched the film thirteen times already, twice with his son Ryan and on many occasions alone at Liberty Cinema—a grand theatre built in the Art Deco style—near Marine Lines, so he could witness Gabbar's death play out on the seventy-mm screen.

The beard apart, Gabbar's swollen eye bags, protruding belly and villainous disposition called to mind his brother-in-law. Not to mention that cruel, rolling laughter that engulfed Bosco Mansion every night after Benjamin got drunk. Michael truly wanted him dead. And considering the number of times he had attended Benjamin's funeral in his dreams, one could only imagine how desperately he had wished for the reality.

That wait ended on 14 February 1976, on the feast of St Valentine. Decades later, this day took on an unholy life of its own when men from a saffron brigade in Bombay went about trampling over the hearts of the city's romantics. They couldn't fathom how a Western idea had won favour among the youth when it was the greatness of their Maratha warrior king, whose birthday followed a few days later, that should have been celebrated. In their politics of hate, they spared no one. They destroyed shops, crushed roses, pulled the cotton out of heart-shaped cushions, and ripped apart cards filled with moving verse. Lovers suffered the most. At Marine Drive, where they sat perilously within the open gaps of the cemented tetra-pods, hanging between life and death to enjoy a private moment of sweetness, they were pulled from each other's embrace abruptly, dragged onto the promenade and beaten to pulp until they swore to never repeat this 'vulgar' show of love again.

V-Day in the city became synonymous with Violence Day. Michael described the slew of unfortunate events as 'the curse of Benjamin', who had chosen to die on this very day.

Death came quietly. Benjamin succumbed to a massive cardiac arrest, just like his enemy, Joe. Only, he had been in a drunken stupor, fast asleep.

Dr Pravin Desai had always thought his patient's ruptured liver would kill him. All the alcohol Benjamin had flushed into his system had done irreparable harm to that organ. The doctor had warned that it could get worse if he did not give up the vice. But Benjamin's life, marriage and upsetting musical career had mostly veered in unpredictable directions. His death wasn't going to be different.

On the morning when Benjamin was found lying motionless in bed, a hysterical Annette had come running down to her brother's flat to break the news. Her relationship with Michael had hit a new low after Joe's death, and they barely spoke. Yet today wasn't the kind of day to hold grudges. To her shock, Michael remained unmoved.

'What do you want me to do?' he asked, indifferent to her sobbing.

'He is dead,' she broke down. 'My husband is dead, and you are asking me what to do. How can you be so stone-hearted?'

'See, I don't know how I can help,' Michael lied. 'If it's money you want, I will have Merlyn send it. I am sure the da Cunhas will want to handle the funeral arrangements.'

Michael didn't mean a single word of what he had said, but hate and anger had been festering within him since Joe's death six years ago. He didn't want to let go of an opportunity to remind his sister that her moment of comeuppance had finally arrived. He succeeded. Annette hadn't expected her brother to react the way he did; she hurled a string of abuses at him and stormed out of his home, banging the door behind her.

'What a bitch!' he murmured. 'Husband has died, but she will still go about banging things in my house.'

'You gone mad re?' Merlyn reprimanded her husband. It was a Saturday; Sarah had gone to work—she was training as an accountant at a bank—and their son had left for college just a few minutes earlier. Worried for her imprudent sister-in-law, she rushed to the kitchen, turned off the fire on the stove and hurried after Annette, who was howling like a madwoman.

While the mood in the Coutinho home had turned sombre, the rest of Cavel was feeling celebratory. It was the seventy-fifth birthday of their dearest priest Fr Augustine Fernandez, who thirty-one years ago had miraculously escaped from the 'fires of hell'.

Fr Augustine had long ceased to be the parish priest of Our Lady of Hope. In 1955, he was transferred to another parish. In the next two decades, he moved three churches between Colaba and Anderi—most Goan Catholics in the city were oblivious to the 'H' in Andheri, just as they were to the 'Ra' in Bandra, choosing to call the suburb Bandruh.

'The parishioners in Anderi keep hoping that he repeats the miracle there,' Joana Misquitta told her friend Ellena during one of their tea-time gossip sessions. 'You know what they did? They kept two huge candles in front of him during the Easter vigil.'

'You aren't telling me they did it deliberately, are you? But wait! Who told you that?'

'Don't you remember Alan Vaz? He is married to a girl from that parish in Marol in Anderi.'

'Yes, yes, I remember. But, oh! That's so horrible,' said Ellena.

'I know, Elle. Imagine putting the priest at risk just for a miracle!'

Fr Augustine was now living in a far-flung village in Vasai. He was spending his retirement years learning Marathi from the local East Indian villagers, while penning a memoir on the life of a priest, who had experienced Jesus' miracle. This, he confessed to Michael, was being written on the insistence of fellow priests who had heard the marvellous Christmas story of 1945.

'It's going to be a tell-all book,' he told Michael, with whom he had shared a close rapport over the years. 'I am going to narrate the truth and put an end to all those rumours. You will edit it, son, won't you?'

What truth? Michael wondered. Fr Augustine himself believed he had been saved from the demon and was on a guilt trip for years because he had skipped a few verses during the Bible reading. If Michael were to edit the book, he would re-write the story entirely. But the lie was too deeply embedded in Cavel's memory to be edited or re-written.

Now that Fr Augustine was turning seventy-five—an extraordinary feat for someone the Cavelites thought should have been dead years ago—he was invited to the church of that little miracle to celebrate a thanksgiving mass. It was to be followed by a get-together of all the parishioners in the compound of Pope's Colony.

The Goan Catholic Club had long been rendered unusable for parties or social gatherings. Though the building was repaired twice, people were too scared to put themselves and their guests at risk. So it now served as a space for Bible sessions, and not more than ten people thronged the hall at any given time. Benjamin da Cunha's Parsi sister-in-law, Perin da Cunha, led the sessions here. She had converted to Catholicism before marrying Hubert fifteen years ago.

When Perin Irani, the fair lady from Dadar Parsi Colony, moved to Cavel, a lot of hearts had skipped multiple beats. She was quite literally a beauty from another world. The obsession with white skin—paklos, as fair-skinned people were called in Konkani—was a trait that came with being Indian and most importantly, Goan. It wouldn't have otherwise taken the Portuguese four hundred years to leave the Indian Catholic heartland.

But Perin was not just white, she was also a looker. It felt as if the gods had worked on every bit of her face very patiently. One could drown in those almond-shaped grey eyes and sink in the long, endless river of her eyebrows and still find a reason to rise and brush against her soft pink lips. And she had to only smile for those cheeks to glow a rosy pink. Then, of course, there was her hourglass figure, never once compromised in her embroidered gara sarees, which she wore only with sleeveless blouses.

Perin no longer drew that kind of attention when she walked down D'Lima Street. Though still pretty, she made little effort now to impress. She ditched those sarees for cotton dresses to hide her thick waist. And she didn't even bother painting her lips anymore. The aristocracy of her past had vanished from her face.

In Cavel, she was now described as the most pious person in the neighbourhood. She made it a point to attend mass each morning on weekdays. On Sundays, she'd spend the entire day in church, teaching the kids at catechism class, attending the Legion of Mary meeting, and practising with the choir for next Sunday's mass.

But this piety took a backseat in the evenings because Perin, like her brother-in-law, had a drinking problem. She had a deep sorrow from which she would only find escape in the bottle. There were days when she'd join Benjamin at the Kit Kat bar, setting rumour mills turning. The possibility of an affair was highly improbable. She enjoyed Benjamin's company because he was the only person who admired her holy ways while also encouraging her recklessness with liquor.

It was Perin who came to Annette's mind when she ran out of her brother's home. Like everyone else, Annette too had believed that her husband and Perin were having an affair. The couple had spent many nights arguing, fighting and screaming their lungs out over this. But in his death, all this was forgiven and forgotten. If Perin really loved him, she would know of her pain, Annette told herself. What she needed right now was a friend to share her grief with, not a brother to mock her choice of husband.

She made a dash for the second floor of Lobo Mansion to meet the da Cunhas, Merlyn a few steps behind her.

Only Perin and Hubert lived in this once over-populated home. Benjamin's parents had died a few years earlier, just six months apart, and the other brothers, over the course of the last ten years, had moved to the suburbs for want of space.

Perin had no children and this was often blamed on her drunken escapades. Nobody, however, knew that her husband was the cause of her distress, not even the parish priest to whom she religiously went for confession every week, unburdening herself and discussing her hundredth failed attempt to abstain from alcohol. Hubert, she had found out, was having an affair with his boss' wife. Hotel rooms were booked weekend after weekend. Perin, who had abandoned both family and faith for this man, was forced to find solace in God first, and when that didn't help, in alcohol.

The two women seemed to have caught Perin at the wrong time. She was busy making chutney sandwiches for Fr Augustine's birthday celebrations in the evening. Around three hundred chicken puffs and chocolate-walnut cake slices were already on their way from her father's Irani bakery. She couldn't conceal her excitement about the evening and was prancing from the dining table to the kitchen, with the butter knife and jar of chutney, unaware of the visitors waiting for her in the drawing room. Shanti, her housemaid, came to call her. 'Annette tai is crying.'

This was routine. Annette had on several occasions in the past come to Lobo Mansion with a litany of complaints about the 'devil-of-a-child' they had raised. Perin assumed that Benjamin had beaten up his wife again. Though annoyed that Annette had disturbed her sandwich-making, Perin rehearsed words of comfort as she made her way out.

What she saw in front of her was a heap of misery. Annette was on the rocking chair, her hair dishevelled and eyes puffed up. Merlyn was on the floor, plying her with platitudes in Konkani.

'Good heavens, what happened? Is that Benji boy drinking in the mornings now?' Perin asked. Even as she said this, she realised she had been complicit in the crime and held back, half embarrassed.

But at least she didn't drink in the mornings, she assured herself.

'He is dead. Our Benji is dead,' Annette cried out, breaking Perin's chain of thought.

'What!' she said, shocked.

'Cardiac arrest,' Merlyn replied.

It took a while before the news could sink in.

'Let me … let me call Hubert,' Perin said.

But suddenly she remembered that her husband was in Lonavla with his lady love and would only arrive in time for Fr Augustine's birthday party. So she added, as if speaking to herself, 'First, I will inform the rest.'

Perin calmly reached for the telephone and swivelled the dial to call Benji's older brother, Anthony. As she spoke with him, Annette couldn't help but notice that Perin didn't seem very affected.

When she put the receiver down, Annette dared to ask, 'Aren't you devastated, Peru? We lost our Benji.'

'I … I am, of course,' Perin said hesitantly, unsure of what to say. 'But your loss is greater.'

By now Annette had lost all her ability to think straight. 'What do you mean, bitch?' she hollered. 'Wasn't it into your drunken arms that he would fall each night? Didn't he spend all of yesterday making love to you while Hubert was away? And now you can't grieve? You can't cry?'

Perin's ears were singeing. Merlyn was aware of the rumours, but never gave them much credence. She was probably as appalled as Perin.

'Oh saiba!' she muttered under her breath.

'I won't tolerate such accusations,' Perin said, her body shaking.

'This is the truth, you bitch,' Annette said. She was all set to jump at Perin but Merlyn held her tight, and with the help of Shanti, dragged her out of the house.

When they left, Perin slumped to the floor. The glass jar of chutney she had been holding fell down and cracked, rolling and spilling a mixture of green all over the ground. The air silently mingled with the pungent smell of a mélange of freshly ground coriander leaves, mint leaves and green chillies. Perin tried to save the chutney from spreading, but a shard of glass from the broken jar pierced the flesh of her ring finger. She let herself bleed, and when she was tired, she took a mound of the spicy paste, now mixed with her own blood, and started to dab it all over her body. Her white skin was flushed and burning.

Her eyes turned moist, but she didn't cry. A few minutes later, she picked herself up, washed and cleaned her wound and went back into the kitchen. She was going to miss Benji, but first she had to make fresh chutney.

The rest of the da Cunha family, which was in any case heading to town for the priest's birthday, thought it made sense to wrap up the funeral as soon as possible so that it didn't affect the momentous celebrations of the evening.

Anthony da Cunha made a quick call to Michael and requested him to reach out to the undertaker in the neighbouring lane of Dabul to make arrangements for the coffin.

'We can't waste time or everything will get delayed,' Anthony told him. Before Michael could hang up, another request came in. 'Could you please also arrange for the obituary in an afternoon paper? Since you are a journalist, it would be easier.'

'See, this is proof. Everybody wants to get rid of that bloody man,' Michael told his wife as he hung up.

'Baba, you don't start re, please,' Merlyn said. She was still recovering from what had happened with Perin. When she told her husband about it, he cursed the life out of his sister.

'Huh! That woman is dragging Perin down now,' he said. 'And who the hell is she to say that? Didn't you see her romping around with Joe in the bazaar?'

'Forget it re …'

'I am warning you, Merlyn, keep away from her. She is bad company.'

Whenever strange things happened in Cavel, Fr Augustine had been at the centre of it. Here he was now in the place of that haunting memory from over three decades ago, where, along with his birthday, a plan for a funeral was underway.

Barely had his driver parked his Padmini outside Our Lady of Hope when he saw Michael come out of the church office.

'Son, long time,' he called out from inside the car. Fourteen years had passed since Michael had last met the priest in person.

The vastness of time had shown itself. Fr Augustine had shrivelled; the creases on his face were stronger and more pronounced.

Their conversations had suffered the blow of distance with letters that were few and far between. Michael's mails were mostly about work and the political events unfolding in the city. For years, Fr Augustine served as an insider to the community, offering Michael a steady supply of news about the goings-on inside the Archdiocese. It was strange that Michael trusted him with information, considering he was convinced that Fr Augustine's miracle was a figment of his own imagination.

Of late though, working for the press had become drab, especially after Prime Minister Indira Gandhi declared the Emergency. It had been months since Michael had reported on politics or religion because everything he wrote was brutally censored anyway. He had even got his bosses at *The Express* to shift him back to the news desk. Editing meaningless copy made work at the newspaper seem bearable. It was better than reporting about all that great work being done by Mrs Gandhi sans criticism and about her changing taste in sarees.

The two exchanged quick pleasantries, after which Michael shared the news that had brought him to church.

'That banjo player, you mean? He died? Oh son! I am so sorry for your loss,' the priest said.

Michael nodded, struggling to not give away the immense joy this development had brought him. 'When's the mass?' Fr Augustine asked.

It so happened that on the day that the parish invited Fr Augustine to celebrate the mass, Fr Jeremy Pereira, the parish priest of Our Lady of Hope, had to urgently leave for Nagpur to see his mother who had taken ill. It was unlikely then that there would be more than one mass in church that day, unless they could make a last-minute arrangement for another priest. The gracious and accommodating Fr Augustine offered to hold the funeral mass at 4 p.m.—the same time as his mass had been scheduled.

News spread like wildfire in Cavel. Parish members were livid that Fr Augustine had thrown cold water on their preparations by deciding to hold a funeral service when they had been planning this thanksgiving mass for months on end.

The choir was trained by Thelma D'Costa, the piano virtuoso who had once given her heart to the hockey superstar Lester Ferreira. Their love story turned into one of the most passionate romances Cavel had ever seen. The pair was inseparable once Lester was discharged from the hospital. People would see them cuddling and kissing in every private corner of the neighbourhood, especially at the foot of the stairs of 185, Monte Building, where Thelma lived. She would sneak out of home late at night and fall into the arms of her lover. He'd fondle her with his large hands, moving his lips frantically all over her body as though he was famished. When Thelma's father, Gabriel Antao D'Costa, caught them red-handed, he plucked his daughter out of this dreamy feasting and locked her in her room for days together.

When tempers cooled, Gabriel's wife urged him to meet Lester and tell him to marry their daughter. 'Before she brings us more shame,' she begged. Lester's response turned Gabriel raving mad.

'I don't believe in the institution of marriage, sir,' Lester maintained.

A heartbroken Thelma never saw Lester again. She decided to give herself completely to music, training young children to discover the magic in their tiny fingers. When Lester's wedding card was delivered to her home a year later, she burnt it along with the many love notes he had written to her, and scattered the ashes in the sea at Marine Drive.

Thelma never married, but she did spend much of her youth building one of the most sonorous choirs in Bombay, comprising a melodic mix of sopranos, altos, bassists and tenors. They called themselves The Jubilants. When not singing in churches across Bombay, they performed at the gymkhanas—the equivalent to sophisticated clubs in other cities—in Marine Lines and Bandra.

For this particular mass, she had chosen some of the finest hymns her choir had ever sung, including one of her own liturgical compositions that she hadn't played before. The news of the change in service upset her plans greatly, as hers wasn't a choir that sang for funerals.

But if Lester hadn't died of leukaemia three months earlier—a relatively new disease then—Thelma would have been far from prepared today. In his last days, Lester wrote to her and requested that she play for him at his funeral.

'There has never been a woman I have loved and cared for more,' he wrote. He never offered an explanation for why he had chosen a life with Valencia Borges, the daughter of one of the leading gynaecologists in the city, over Thelma. But then, Thelma never wanted the answer. She attended Lester's funeral, and The Jubilants sang, giving a fitting tribute to one of Bombay's greatest sporting legends.

'We will sing the same hymns again,' she informed her choir.

'That Benji bugger doesn't deserve us,' Tony, the lead singer, spoke up.

'Neither did Lester,' Thelma pointed out. Tony knew better than to argue.

How does one explain how the notorious look when dead? Placed in a plywood coffin in a grey-striped suit that he had had made in the prime of his youth when he performed only for Bombay's glitziest, Benjamin alias Benji alias Banjo Man shared no resemblance to the evil and ugly soul that he had been yesterday. He looked peaceful. But if you looked closely, you'd notice that his lips had a faint curl to them from the shock of dying, as if even to him, death had come by surprise.

Benji didn't have a pleasant face. He could have once been considered charming, but years of insobriety had stolen that spark from his eyes, leaving them permanently swollen, red and menacing. The binge drinking also led to an odd disfigurement, and as he lay still in his coffin, his shape looked even more revolting. Force fitted into the suit, the tyres of his belly strained against the fabric and threatened to burst out any moment.

As Annette fitted a rosary into the tiny depression of her husband's intertwined fingers, she couldn't fathom that this was the man she had shared her first kiss with. He who had promised her the stars and the moon, had taught her only what it was to be in hell every day. Yet, there was nobody else her heart felt so much compassion and affection for. What would her life have been like if she had married Joe instead? Could she have thus saved the living from dying and the dying from death? She knew nothing now. A widow of fate and her own choices, it would be a long time before Annette would reconcile herself to the fact that she had killed two men with one impulsive decision. She drew closer to Benjamin's swollen face, which had not had a shave in weeks, wanting to leave him with a kiss on his lips, but she left a peck on his chin instead. Benjamin's mouth was still stinking from the previous night's binge.

The church hadn't seen such a huge congregation in decades. The balcony, which was otherwise locked as the choir now sang from near the altar, had to be thrown open. Many Cavelites who had moved to the suburbs and even Goa had returned to celebrate the glorious symbol of God's miracle. People had turned out in their best clothes. Red, blue, ochre, pink. Bell-bottoms, polka-dot shirts, miniskirts and satin flairs. These colours and cuts were meant for a feast. Only now, in an unlikely turn of events, the congregation was forced to sit through a funeral service instead. If they were sad, it was for Fr Augustine, who they believed didn't deserve this fate. 'The devil always tries to have his way,' they told each other.

After mass, people grudgingly queued up to give their condolences to the Coutinhos and da Cunhas before joining another line to greet their beloved priest. By the time the family members had placed the coffin in the hearse and prepared to leave for St Peter's Cemetery in Haines Road, Worli, it was already 5.30 p.m. Most of the parishioners were making their way to the compound for the festivities.

The priest too excused himself from attending the burial, having surmised that the majority of the congregation had been unhappy with his decision to hold the funeral service during the thanksgiving mass.

'I am sorry, son,' he told Michael. 'But you will understand, I hope.'

There were many who, out of sheer goodwill, joined the family in the bus that was to go to the cemetery.

While getting into the vehicle, Michael noticed Perin, her Bible in hand, walk ahead towards the compound. Hubert, who had returned from Lonavla just in time for the mass, followed her hastily. From this distance, he could see Hubert reach for her arm, and pull Perin towards the bus. A scuffle ensued and Perin shoved her elbow into Hubert's chest. Michael hoped nobody else had seen this spectacle.

When Hubert returned, a curious Michael went to his seat and asked if all was well.

'Peru won't be joining us,' Hubert said, ashen-faced.

'Why?'

'She has to distribute chutney sandwiches,' he said, embarrassed, and turned his head towards the window.

Two hours later, when the bus rolled back into the narrow lane of Dr D'Lima Street and parked outside the compound, the celebration was in full swing. It was a mega carnival of a kind that Cavel had never seen. You couldn't tell that, only a few hours ago, a funeral had taken place here.

Mama Karen, whose mind had, for some time now, been playing tricks, seemed rather sober today. She, along with

Merlyn and her grandkids, caught hold of the grieving Annette and walked her through the milling crowd that made a sudden show of empathy.

'Sorry for your loss,' people kept repeating. Michael remained to chat with a few old-time residents.

Not very far away, somebody was yelling out numbers in a housie game.

'Ulta-pulta sixty-nine.' 'Two fat ladies eighty-eight.' 'Just pass thirty-five.' 'Sweet sixteen.'

Oohs and aahs followed. A ten-year-old had ticked the first numbers and was cheering loudly for herself.

'Jaldi five taken,' the caller said after checking the little girl's ticket. 'Now watch your ticket for the top line, bottom line, middle row and full-house. Big prizes follow,' he went on.

'C'mon, shake the numbers up,' a man yelled. Everyone broke into laughs.

At the steps of Bosco Mansion, the mourning family was obstructed by a group of female performers invited from South Goa for the event. They were decked in gold jewellery and dressed in the traditional pano bhaju, the Goan outfit comprising a long garment wrapped like a sarong (pano) and worn with a loose gold-embroidered blouse (bhaju) and a stole called tuvalo in Konkani. The outfit went back several centuries to a time when the Portuguese insisted that converts adapt to the European style of dressing. The orthodox Brahmin women had found a middle ground, incorporating a few Western sensibilities into their own. The dolled-up ladies were rehearsing Goan mandos, popular Konkani songs of love and longing, which they would soon perform in the middle of the compound. When they saw the family approach, they apologised for blocking the stairs and scattered. Once the Coutinhos had taken the stairs, they regrouped and started singing again.

Up ahead, on a makeshift stage, the Cavel band led by Peter Rodrigues and friends was playing the neighbourhood's most popular jingle: 'Cavel, Cavel such a lovely smell. In the corner rings the church bell, and the crowd begins to swell. Oh! Cavel, Cavel and its beautiful belles ...'

Folks had gathered to join the baan dance, which was quintessentially Cavel. The neighbourhood invented it in the late 1930s or so, after one of its residents attended a ballroom class in London and found inspiration for a new choreography.

Some twenty-odd couples filed into two lines—the ladies in one row and the men in the other—to face each other. As Peter's song picked up pace, the first pair held hands and then separated to go around in circles, twisting, shaking and circling around the others in the line, before returning to each other at the farthest end. The next pair followed them.

Hubert found himself in the thick of this party. He swayed and danced alone.

11

TO LIVE IN THE SKY

January 2010

Some things never changed in Cavel, just like the clinking of the cycle bell every evening at 5.45, heralding the arrival of Mr Paowallah from Daanish's 5 Star Bakery in Girgaum. He brought with him an assortment of breads, khaaris and nankhatais in tarpaulin bags balanced on the handlebar, emptying them one at a time as he knocked on the doors of his patrons.

Since a new person was tasked with this job every few years or so, the residents of Cavel did not feel the need to learn the names of Daanish's breadmen. Rather, very unimaginatively, they gave them the title of Mr Paowallah. Pao was, in fact, an unpopular sobriquet the Goans had earned for themselves among the locals because of their obsession with the soft, chewy buns they ate each morning for breakfast, with everything from butter to marinated curries from the night before—kal chi kodi, as they called them.

When Mr Paowallah arrived this evening, Michael Coutinho was still asleep on his rocking chair. On most days, his afternoon siesta did not extend beyond the stipulated twenty minutes. But the nippy weather had permitted the transgression this time.

On the first day of the New Year, Pope's Colony, once buzzing during the festive season, was dead silent. After Lobo Mansion was brought down last November, and its residents moved to a cushy high-rise in suburban Malad, life in the compound reached a lull. The remaining residents of Cavel, some of whom continued to occupy flats in Bosco, were either absent in flesh and blood, or as good as not around.

No one, for instance, had heard from Ellena in a while. She lived in Goa, but had cut all contact with Cavel. Even her close friends, the Misquittas, only received a greeting card once every year for Christmas, in which she grudgingly shared details of the idyllic life she enjoyed in her village.

Mario, now a sexy septuagenarian, was travelling the world; the money continued to come in from the crosswords he made for an international magazine and the puzzle workshops he conducted globally for enthusiasts. He had last written to Michael a few months earlier, after his thirty-something girlfriend in London had left him for a 'filthy-rich English bugger'.

'F**k her! I've found another doll in Athens. You'll like her too. Wink, wink!' Mario had scrawled on a postcard that showed off the picturesque Greek island of Poros, with its white-washed homes and cerulean sea.

The only other family at Bosco, the Braganzas, whose four children had once driven Ellena stark raving mad with the ruckus they created at playtime, had now sobered. The kids were all grown up and studious, spending fewer hours getting their hands and feet dirty in the playground. Biology had taken precedence over football for Christabell's twins Shanon and Sherwin, both of whom were keen on a career in medicine. Thirteen-year-old Shawn was a professional chess player. And little Sharon, whom Michael had taught to cycle, found herself in the thick of a tight activity schedule, shuttling between French, ballet and piano classes.

Michael himself, just a year shy of eighty but still not crippled by age, once again became a family man, thanks to his sister Annette, who moved into his home two Christmases earlier, after being psyched by the quarrelling ghosts of her husband, Benji, and former lover, Joe.

'These men have taken over my home, men. I don't have a moment of relief. You turn left, they are there. You turn right, and, Jesus, they are still there. Oh God, baba! What do I do?' she asked Michael over the phone.

The spirits, Annette believed, had started bothering her after she stopped visiting their graves. 'I think they got very upset,' she said. 'But they should also understand. How can they expect an old lady to travel all the way to that cemetery in Mahalaxmi? And these taxis, how much they charge, men. They should also understand, no?' she continued, though Michael clearly wasn't listening.

The haunting first began in her bedroom, when Annette woke up one sunny morning to find the ghosts jostling for space on her bed. She even hurt herself during the struggle, as one of them—she couldn't be sure which—tried to push her off the bed.

Next, she saw them in the kitchen, where they attempted to dunk each other's face in the vessel of milk that she had set to boil. Her most humiliating experience, however, was when they came after her in the toilet and fought to catch a glimpse of her bum as she squatted on her haunches. She clutched the skirt that she had lifted to her waist for dear life, watching the drama play out one punch at a time, even as she continued to shit loose bricks out of fear. When she finally found the courage to wash up and run out, the men came after her into the drawing room and wouldn't leave until she promised to choose between the two of them.

'Imagine! I had to say which bhoot is best,' she said. That day, she slept on the sofa and fortunately, they spared her in her dreams.

'Delusional hag,' her brother told her.

'For Christ's sake, believe me for once, baba!'

'Believe you? You do realise that right now you sound just as stupid as my dead wife?' he said, having been reminded of the tantrik episode from over twelve years ago. 'Better go and visit some shrink. Don't chew my brains.'

'Don't you dare say that, okay? Your wife may have been crazy. Not me,' Annette snapped.

Michael realised that the remark had stung. To avoid an argument he had zero patience for, he tried to switch topics, but the blood was already racing through his sister's veins; she cut him short and began blasting him over the phone. 'What would you do without me, huh? Your kids don't give a damn about you. The only one who felt sorry for you, poor dear Laxmi ... you drove her away. It was I ... it was I.' She paused. '... Who took care of you all this while. Now it's time for you to look after me.'

'Wait, what?' Michael asked, confused.

Before he could make sense of the conversation, she said, 'I'm coming down to live with you.'

Michael mumbled something in feeble protest, but she had already slammed the receiver down. And so, just like that, Annette moved into her brother's home on the ground floor, two suitcases in tow. She never left again.

The hallucinations continued, and Michael would often find his sister talking to three men, including himself, at the dining table. It was disturbing when she'd tell him how Joe had undone the drawstrings of his pants when Michael had been fast asleep—and it was true, somebody had loosened them, though he suspected it was his fibbing sister—or how Benji had sipped some whisky from his glass when he wasn't looking. Each time, when recalling these exchanges with her dead lovers, she'd guffaw psychotically, so hard that Michael feared she'd gag on her words. He contemplated getting her psychiatric help, but living off the measly stipend that he made from writing political columns for newspapers, he didn't think it was wise to spend anything on his ungrateful sister. Also, though he hated to admit it, he was enjoying this delusionary company that Annette had brought along with her. His flat felt like a madhouse again.

Tring, tring, tring, trinnnnng. Mr Paowallah was outside the Coutinho residence, merrily going at their doorbell.

Michael, woken by the buzz, hollered at his sister. 'That bloody Paowallah. I'm going to get rid of him along with you very soon.'

Unperturbed by his vacuous threats, which were now routine, Annette, who had started imagining herself as the boss of the house, calmly put down the book she was reading.

Throwing a nasty look at her groggy brother, she headed for the door.

The steel latch at the Coutinhos' home was perennially jammed, and only Michael knew his way around its rusted lock. Annette always struggled for a few minutes, and this annoyed her to the hilt.

'*Kitne baar bola* not to ring that bell, Mr Paowallah! Do it again and Michael uncle will come out with his dandi and *bhagao* you,' she told the person on the other side of the door as she fiddled with the knob.

When she managed to open the door, a young man in his late teens was standing in front of her. He was wearing an oversized black T-shirt over a pair of distressed denims, with every strand of his hair meticulously gelled to stand upright. The anomaly was the loaf of sliced bread and slabs of kadak pao he was holding in both hands.

'And who are you, my child?' Annette asked, surprised.

'Ramesh Paowallah's son,' he said, his mouth twisting and turning as he chewed on gum. He showed absolutely no sign of remorse for having disturbed the old lady by ringing the bell incessantly.

'Where's Mr Paowallah?' Annette enquired.

'Village,' he responded indifferently.

'Achcha. Next time, no ringing the bell, okay? Or Michael uncle …'

'… will *bhagao* me with the dandi. I got it, aunty. Chill pill,' the boy said, trying to imitate her accent, and broke into a laugh, before handing over the bread and running to the top floor.

'These young boys today. No manners only!' Annette muttered, infuriated, and slammed the door.

'Did you warn that bugger?' Michael asked, when he saw her come in with the bread.

'Arre, you're going nuts, men, and you will make me mad with you!' Annette barked. Michael was amused that such a statement had come from her.

'I can't go picking fights with these paowallahs. Anyway, his son came today. I told him not to ring that doorbell again, and you know what he did—he laughed at me, men. Idiot! What does that oversmart kid think of himself? Let Mr Paowallah return, see what I will do.'

There were days when Annette sounded just like her mum. Her mannerisms, her opinions, how she quibbled and the way she spoke, ending sometimes with 'men'—a word that has been part of the Goan lexicon since time immemorial and used for punctuating effect instead of a comma, full-stop, exclamation or question mark—and the way she looked down at people from the pedestal of perfection, everything reminded Michael of his mother. And now, here she was, losing her mind, just like Karen.

'Nice kid. I already like him,' Michael sniggered, recalling how his father would respond to his mum's eccentricities—mostly amused, but always with derision.

Irritated, Annette chucked the newspaper-wrapped pao on the side table and was about to make a dash for the kitchen when she noticed a brightly coloured photograph on the newsprint.

In the picture was an ultra-modern rectangular balcony jutting out of a glass tower, which showed off the stunning view of a vast patch of green land. Standing at the edge, with one hand resting on the glass railing and the other holding a mug of coffee, was a seventy-something woman soaking in the sprawling landscape in front of her. Below this picture, in a curly font, were the words: 'Live in the sky before it's time.'

Had it not been for the subject of the picture, Annette would have ignored this hyperbolic newspaper advertisement, which was trying very hard to be affecting and moving at the cost of being insensitive to a woman her age. But how could she ignore the face of this woman? She looked eerily familiar.

Annette picked up the sheet of paper and took it to Michael, who was still slightly woozy from the long nap.

'What happened now?' he asked, as he saw her pale face.

She handed him the newspaper and pointed to the picture. 'Is this her?'

Michael didn't need more than a few seconds to recognise the person in the photograph.

'Peru,' he whispered.

Residents of Pope's Colony had last seen Perin before Benjamin's funeral on the evening of 14 February 1976. Rumour was that she was so traumatised by the news of her lover's death that she decided to leave Cavel all at once. Her husband, Hubert, who couldn't believe she would abandon him, and sister-in-law Annette, who thought Perin had been sharing her husband and bed, only added fuel to the fire. Thirty-four years later, here she was, happily staring into the abyss like nothing had ever happened.

'I must say … this lady has aged gracefully,' said Michael, gazing at the photograph in awe.

Perin looked plumper than he could recall, but neither time nor age had robbed her of that smile he could see on her face. If there were a few creases on the milk-white skin of her face, they were hidden by the pink of her cheeks. She seemed content. Even her gold-rimmed spectacles couldn't contain the gleam in her eyes. She was flaunting one of those gara sarees that harked back to the days before she married into the da Cunha household. She was deliberately under-dressed to look like an old Parsi granny, and the ad said so too: 'At 74, Meher Irani, a grandma of two, is finally living her dream.'

'How can she look so happy?' Annette demanded as she pored over the ad.

'What do you mean?' Michael said.

'She has no right to be happy. See what she did to that poor Hubert, men. He died alone because of her,' Annette said. 'And now she's showing off … granny and all.'

'Oh, please! We all know what that Hubert was up to. Bloody romping around with his boss' wife till she had no use for him.'

'That's not true. You know Benji was having an affair with her?'

'In your dreams, he was, yes. Peru had standards, mind you,' Michael growled.

'Oh! Peru and all, huh? I won't be surprised if she gave you a good time too. Did your woman know?'

That was when Michael lost his cool. 'Bitch, you are crossing the line,' he hollered.

'Do me a favour. Stop opening that foul mouth of yours,' Annette snapped and dashed straight for the bedroom, locking it from the inside.

Michael could hear her howl. He knew that the photograph of Peru looking so outrageously happy had sparked feelings of inadequacy and insecurity in Annette. He couldn't care less. He was glad Perin had saved herself from a hopeless marriage and had chosen to live in the sky, even if it was for a print advertisement.

Annette didn't come out of the room that entire evening. At half past nine, when the door to his son's room still remained shut, Michael, who wasn't going to allow his sister's tantrums to cause a hunger crisis at home, called up Custodio D'Silva and ordered a fish curry.

Custodio lived in the lane across from Bosco Mansion, in 181 Cross Gully, which continued to house a chunk of Cavel's Goan Catholic population. The families there lived in cramped quarters, with no well-defined space for a kitchen, bathroom or even a bed in which to make love. It was this absence of basic comforts that made them seek a better life more aggressively. This explained why the most enterprising and hardworking of the lot from Cavel—the teachers at some of the best convent schools, the mechanics at the high-end garages and cooks at the city's finest caterers and hotels—hailed from here. Yet, despite their best efforts to rescue themselves from the small life, Michael remembered how, in the early years, the elders at Pope's Colony would look down upon the people from Cross Gully, discouraging any kind of friendship—romance in particular—with them. In her lifetime, aunty Tresa was punched into this category, stigmatised by so many, including his mum, much to Michael's irritation. 'A woman of the chawls,' Karen called Tresa, unimpressed by her attempts to find a 'decent' livelihood to survive.

Michael had always disdained the classists from Bosco and Lobo Mansions, who considered themselves to be of another breed of humanity just because their homes were larger and their ancestors wealthier or famous. What most of them ended up doing with their lives, Benji and his sister included, was pure tragedy.

It was no surprise then that Michael had more friends from Cross Gully than Pope's Colony. Among the people whose company he enjoyed was Custodio. The sixty-five-year-old used to be the head chef on a cruise ship and retired a few years ago to start a food service out of his home, preparing a variety of piquant Goan fish curries, mutton stews and pork vindaloos each morning that went to people across South Mumbai. Though he stopped taking orders by 6 p.m., he'd never refuse Michael's request to send him some leftover ambotik, a Goan fish curry made with red chillies and tamarind juice, always adding an extra piece or two of the head of the mackerel, which Michael savoured most.

When the food parcel arrived at 10 p.m., Michael was too hungry to worry about anything else in the world, especially his sister. He got out a plate from the kitchen and sat at the table. He tore into his kadak pav and had started soaking it in the tangy fish curry when he heard the bedroom door open. Annette crept into the dining hall, her eyes bloodshot from all the crying.

'Eat something,' Michael said, trying hard to sound courteous, but actually irritated that he'd now have to share his fish. She didn't say no—as expected—and sat down next to him. That night, they enjoyed their meal quietly. Annette's ghost friends didn't interrupt for a change. Michael had to admit that it was one of the most peaceful dinners he had had in a while.

The following morning, frantic sounds from Annette's room stirred Michael from his slumber. It was 6 a.m., too early for visitors to be bothering them. He climbed out of bed and tiptoed out, inching closer to the door of her room to eavesdrop on the conversation. When he was within earshot, he could hear his sister's voice loud and clear: 'Benji, are you sure?'

She paused, as if to listen to someone, and then spoke again, 'Yes, even I don't agree with Joe. But don't you think we should wait?'

Again, there was a brief silence before she continued, 'You are actually right, men. I get you. Let me speak to baba.'

Of course, the ghosts had returned, Michael thought to himself as he walked back to his room, sleep-deprived. He was already dreading what was to follow. What were the two idiots planning together? Why did the mad couple not agree with Joe, he wondered as he rested his head on the pillow. Before his mind could spin more questions, he fell asleep.

Three hours later, Annette came into his room with a hand-written sheet of paper in her hand. He had woken up sometime earlier and was lying in bed, staring at the fan whirring slowly above him. On seeing her, he remembered the conversation he had overheard in the morning and decided not to encourage her. Behaving as if she wasn't in his line of vision, Michael lifted himself out of bed and took slow steps out of the room, heading for the toilet. She followed him closely as his ageing feet staggered through the hallway. He considered himself lucky to still not need a stick.

'Baba ... baba, we have to talk,' she said, walking behind him.

'What's it about?' he asked, refusing to stop.

'We have something to discuss,' she said.

'Who is we?'

'Me and Benji,' she responded, as if the existence of her dead husband was the most normal thing in the world.

'It's about this building,' she continued, even though Michael hadn't asked her to.

'Hmm …'

'I feel we should move out.'

'Who is this we again?' he asked, wary of what she was about to say.

'You and I, and everyone else in this building. We should go and stay in a tall building. You know, like how everyone at Lobo's did!'

'And you have decided that for all of us?' he questioned nonplussed.

'No, Benji and I.'

'You know who really needs to move out?'

She didn't respond. She knew what was coming.

'You and your bloody Benji. Your idiot husband, he makes me want to fart. Now get out of my way. I need to shit,' Michael said and shut the toilet door.

The century-old Bosco Mansion had been in the eye of a storm ever since the residents of Lobo, afraid that their decrepit building would soon give away, agreed with their landlord to sell the property to a developer—a notorious goon. They settled amicably, but for peanuts. While a massive forty-storey building was expected to come up where Lobo Mansion used to be, the former residents accepted homes half the size of their original flats in the suburban area of Malad, nearly thirty kilometres from Cavel. Malad boasted a church with tens of thousands of parishioners, making the shift out of shrinking Cavel more lucrative.

The ten residents of Lobo, convinced about the bright future that awaited them, quietly left for their new abodes, leaving friends at Bosco stranded. But Michael and Mario, and Christabell's husband Shane Braganza, the new secretary of the association formed by the Bosco residents, were determined to not be short-changed by the greedy developer or pressured by the landlord, who'd been harassing them ever since Lobo Mansion was sold.

It's true that 193-A, Bosco Mansion was withering away—the Burma teak rotting from years of neglect. Only a few years earlier, in 2005, on the day the city had drowned in a horrifying deluge, Annette's kitchen window fell into Michael's garden. Some days later, during another downpour, part of a beam supporting her balcony collapsed and crushed the windshield of eighty-nine-year-old widow Rose Maria's Fiat Padmini. The sky-blue car had been out of use for nearly fourteen years, but Rose, who had purchased it for Joe immediately after they were married, didn't have the heart to sell or get rid of it. Annette apologised to her and also promised to have the car repaired. But two days later, Rose died of a sudden bout of fever. It was as if her soul had clung to the car all this while.

Rose didn't have anyone to call family. So the Catholic trust decided to seal her property till they found a new tenant with whom they'd sign a contract, giving them possession rights under the Rent Control Act. One had to be foolish to put one's money in such an old home. No tenant came. Meanwhile, the car remained for many, many months—rotting, rusting and changing from blue to grey to dull brown, becoming another spooky source of entertainment in the locality.

The Braganza kids first fanned the rumour that the ghost of Rose had taken her car for a spin inside the compound late at night. Children from Lobo Mansion joined in the fun. Soon, other youngsters from the nearby Pius and Monte buildings, as well as Cross Gully, began spreading their own stories. Late one night, when nobody was watching, a bunch of naughty teens from Cross Gully sneaked into Pope's Colony and spray-painted the car with the words: 'If you touch it, my ghost will kill you.'

One of the more artistically inclined boys even painted a danger sign with a skeleton that looked eerily like Rose. Michael had had enough. He called the raddiwallah and paid him one thousand rupees to dump the car.

'What you doing re, Mike … you paying the fellow money for the car. He must pay you, na? He will get so much money from this raddi,' Merlyn said, upset with his generosity.

'If I don't get rid of this car, Bosco will become a bhoot bangla,' he chided her.

But a few years later, Bosco did turn into a ghost town of sorts, where not even the residue of its glorious years lingered.

When Michael got out of the toilet twenty minutes later, his sister was still waiting patiently for him near the door.

'What's your problem?' he asked as he ambled out.

'Listen to me,' she pleaded.

Because he didn't react, she continued, 'You know, Benji was very sad this morning. He came to tell me sorry about having that affair with Perin. He is a changed man now, baba, and has promised to make up for all the hurt he caused me and his brother.'

Michael rolled his eyes.

'He said, "Ann, you also have the right to be happy like Perin,"' she continued.

'Aah!' Michael interrupted. 'And he told you to shift to a high-rise.'

She nodded. 'But this Joe doesn't agree, men. He thinks we are too old to relocate. Benji gave him a good scolding. One is never really too old for anything, no?'

'So go! Who is stopping you? Give up your flat and leave,' Michael said indifferently as he made his way to the kitchen to pour himself some of the tea Annette made each morning.

'No tea today?' he asked when he saw an empty pot on the gas stove.

Choosing not to respond to that, Annette went on, 'Baba, who will buy the house now? It's so old. I think we should just tell that developer that we want to move. He will find us a good home in Malad.'

'I am not going anywhere.'

She ignored him. 'I called your kids in the morning. They think I am right.'

'Who are they to decide what's good for me?' he asked.

'Don't forget, baba, their names are in your will and mine, too. They have equal say.'

'Done your homework, have you?'

'More than you think,' she taunted. 'I also met Shane and Christabell in the morning.'

'That's why you didn't make tea today?' Michael asked.

'I am not your servant,' she said. 'I told them that we should at least consider any offer the developer makes us. Shane told me he'd fix a meeting with the landlord and developer if you are keen too.'

'No way,' Michael barked.

'Most of us want it, baba. I have your kids, Benji and the Braganzas on my side. You just have Joe,' Annette said confidently. 'Shane will convince the rest.'

'Benji and Joe are dead, you stupid lady,' Michael snapped.

She obviously needed to get her head examined, Michael thought to himself. But before that, he had a lot of work on his hands, including getting more people on his side. This meant reaching out to Mario and Ellena. Nobody would know where Mario was until the arrival of his next postcard. Michael owned a second-hand Macbook, one that his son, Ryan, had left behind for him the last time he visited. When he learnt that his father still typed out his columns and couriered them, Ryan warned him that he'd soon run out of a good occupation unless he kept up with the times. This was the only occasion when Michael listened to Ryan, having previously refused his son's offer to help improve his bank balance.

The laptop had since then only existed for the purpose of shooting columns to editors. He wasn't sure if Mario had an email ID of his own. It was likely that he did, and if so, Shane would try and reach out to him to let him know of the development.

Michael had heard of the big secrets of Google but was always averse to digging into the web. Today, he risked its use, searching for 'Mario "King" Lawrence, *The London Times*'.

Mario had acquired the title during his heyday as a crossword-maker; it became a permanent fixture when he got himself a passport. Google threw up interesting results. Fortunately, the newspaper Michael worked for had created for him a contributor's email ID for reader feedback. He immediately shot off a mail to Mario. The subject was very pointed: 'We need to save Bosco, come back.'

It had been six years since Mario returned to Mumbai. The last time was for his mother's funeral. Michael wasn't sure when he'd hear from him last, but right now, he had a bigger hurdle to overcome—that of convincing Ellena Gomes to return.

It wasn't like he had not tried to reconnect with her. But not with another letter, because he wasn't sure what he could say. Instead, he tried calling her. But her landline number from over two-and-a-half years ago was disconnected. Michael even contemplated going all the way to Goa to meet her in the hope that they'd reconcile. He really missed the friendship they had shared in those months of exchanging letters. And he really missed her. The letters—none of their kind had ever been written to him by any woman, not even his wife—meant something to him. They were a collection of loving memories, arguments, reconciliations and confessions he didn't have the courage to part with. Yet, there was also his wife, Merlyn, the woman he had spent a significant time of his life loving and knowing and who meant so much more to him than Ellena could. He could tell the difference, and so he had held himself back in his letters to Ellena each time.

Michael found out from their neighbours that Ellena hadn't moved to a new place yet. She still lived in her family home in Pernem. Maybe he should write to her. But what could he say without sounding like he was once again being selfish, reaching out to her only in his time of need? He twiddled his fingers the entire day, catching flashes of his sister swinging from one room to another like she had bagged an Olympic gold. It was only later that night, after Annette had gone to sleep, that he picked up his pen for the first time in many years to write to Ellena.

Dearest Butterfly, he wrote, and suddenly realising that it was highly inappropriate, scratched it out. *Dearest Ellena*. No, not working either, he told himself. *Dear Ellena* would be better. He took out a fresh sheet of paper and wrote, *Hi Ellena …*

Hours turned into days and days into weeks, but Michael didn't hear from her. Meanwhile, Mario had written back almost immediately, spelling out clearly in his email, which was copied to Shane as well as the trustees, that he would use all his 'might and money' to ensure that the building didn't 'go to the dogs'. Two emails followed soon after—again copied to all the parties concerned—one announcing that he was to land in Mumbai on 28 January, and the other that he had already found a lawyer who would be representing Michael and him.

Shane, who, until then, was only mulling the idea of redevelopment, was suddenly emboldened to pursue the issue. He hated the guts of these 'two old wily men', and decided to take them head-on. In a nasty email, he said, 'In the event of you planning to go to court, I have my own posse of lawyers and officials who will show you your rightful place.'

The landlord, only too happy to sell this old property, fanned the flames further, claiming that as per law, the final decision would rest with the majority.

Team Shane and Team Michael were ready for battle. The former comprised Annette, the Braganzas and Michael's kids. The latter was too insignificant to even be considered a spot of bother. Desperate to save his home, Michael wrote to his kids, threatening to write them out of his will. He didn't mean it, but if push came to shove, he planned to use this threat very seriously. How could they deny him the one thing he expected of them—his happiness?

Michael wasn't averse to change, but he also believed in the permanence of some things, especially his hearth and home. Yet, his stubbornness had kept him from enjoying and exploring the small pleasures of newness, like his beautiful friendship with Ellena.

There was another reason he held on to this home so steadfastly. Every person he had loved—his parents, his childhood sweetheart, his best friend, his wife—had been connected to this building in some way or the other. He could feel the residual energy of their souls, the lingering of their warmth and conversations within the confines of Bosco's walls. It brought him comfort when everything else around him seemed to be crumbling. He saw no reason to rot in a high-rise apartment just because his crazy sister wanted to prove to another lady that she could be as happy as she.

Mario arrived from London on the morning of 28 January, just three days before the fate of the residents of Bosco was to be sealed at a meeting in the landlord's office. While Michael suggested that Mario stay at his place—as his home needed cleaning—within a few hours, it became apparent that Mario would flee sooner than planned. Annette was yapping away at full volume with her ghost friends, bitching about having to cook for the nuisance-of-a-guest, which made him feel very unwelcome.

By dinner time, Mario was already tired of her antics, and he stepped out with Michael to the compound to catch some fresh air. It had been a while since Michael had dared to go out in the dark, but he needed some quiet time just as much as Mario did.

The two walked under the white glow of the tube-light installed at the entrance of the building. 'Ann is super crazy,' Mario said as they walked towards the gate at Pope's Colony. 'And I thought I was the only person who had a problem,' he chuckled. After a brief pause, he added, 'You know, some years ago, I was diagnosed with bipolar disorder.'

Michael looked at him, slightly clueless.

'I have these … how do I explain … bouts of highs and lows,' Mario explained.

'Like a mood disorder?' Michael asked.

'Yes. Yes.'

'But didn't you always have it?'

'It was never diagnosed correctly,' Mario said. 'This is more severe. There are days when I feel like I am sinking in a wormhole. And then, on other days, I am alive, flying. You can't catch me. Today in London, tomorrow in Ukraine …'

'So the good days are very good, isn't it?' Michael asked.

'Naa… there is nothing great about living life in such extremes.'

'I am sorry, this is all new to me, Mario.'

'Aah, no. I don't care too much about it.'

'You think Annette… she has this polar thing also?' Michael enquired.

'Bipolar …' Mario corrected.

'Yes, bipolar.'

'Oh no! Your sister is just real mad.' They both broke into a fit of laughter.

'Have you heard from Ellena? My lawyer says she is our only hope,' Mario said when they had covered a considerable distance.

'No,' Michael responded dejectedly.

'That woman has never been helpful.'

Michael chose not to respond to that and continued to walk quietly—the silence between the two was not awkward, just companionable.

While skirting the edge of the compound that directly faced their building, Mario noticed something strange about Bosco Mansion. The light bulb on the balcony of the first floor was flickering nonstop. As they inched closer to the building, they saw someone slowly come out from inside the house and switch off the light before going swiftly back in.

'Are you sure these ghosts are only in Annette's head?' Mario asked, surprised.

'It can't be … it can't be,' Michael said, shocked. 'Butterfly is back.'

12

BOMBAY BALCHÃO

June 2010

They were home finally. Michael. Ellena. Annette. Mario. And the ghosts of Joe and Benjamin. Isn't this what you call the circle of life? An infinite loop that carries people, their memories and stories, and goes round and round before briefly making a halt at some place familiar? In this case, it was 193-A, Bosco Mansion in Pope's Colony on Dr D'Lima Street.

Four months had passed since the day that Annette's dreams of living in the sky with the ghosts of her lovers came to nought. The tenants of three houses opposed the decision to shift. 'We are not giving up our homes at any cost,' Ellena Gomes had announced to the landlord, Neal Pinto, at the meeting that took place at his office in Colaba in early February.

'I renewed my lease in the 1970s. I have occupancy rights like any licensed tenant, and so do the residents of every flat here. I believe you are quite taken by the idea of making money out of your old properties, Mr Pinto, but what are you doing with all that rent we've been giving your trust for donkey's years? You probably have over a crore in your kitty, but not once have you bothered to repair or restore this structure,' Ellena said. 'We can take you to court.'

The slight tremble in her voice had nothing to do with age. It was anger.

Michael and Mario listened, their mouths agape. The lady had done her homework.

Like many homes in the city that were built in the early half of the twentieth century, Bosco Mansion was governed by tenancy laws under the Bombay Rents' Hotel and Lodging House Rates Control Act, 1947, popularly known as the Bombay Rent Act. This law froze rents to a bare minimum. But as property prices began to escalate in the city, maintenance costs spiralled too. With such low rents, it became impossible for landlords to make any profits from these properties, let alone repair them. Over the years, property owners made several appeals in court to revoke the law, but the life of the act continued to be extended. When the Maharashtra Rent Control Act of 1999 finally replaced this archaic law, the rents of tenanted buildings were increased, but by negligible amounts. This put off many owners from looking after their properties. Their buildings would eventually give way, having suffered the neglect of time and an ill-conceived law.

But Bosco Mansion was different. Thanks to its sturdy teakwood foundation, the now hundred-and-five-year-old building had never required maintenance, except once, when a few roof tiles had to be changed. Problems only started emerging some years earlier when the building developed minor cracks, causing a beam to collapse. The landlord, however, turned a blind eye to the issue and the residents were forced to spend money from their own pockets to undertake repair work.

It wasn't a lie that the Catholic Fellowship Trust, which owned nearly ten properties in South Mumbai, including Bosco Mansion, was accumulating the rent in a fixed deposit for aeons, allowing it to slowly multiply. Not even a fraction of it was used to maintain the building. If the trust were to argue a case citing lack of funds for repair or maintenance, it was bound to lose.

Pinto, a forty-five-year-old pot-bellied Goan, had taken over as chairman of this trust—started by his great-grandfather in 1903—around twelve years ago. Greed was second nature to him. For lack of a good occupation, Neal was constantly eyeing newer ways to make money out of his existing family wealth. But Ellena had caught him off-guard. He gulped down a glass of water nervously.

'Are you done, Ms Gomes?' he asked when he had found his bearings.

'No, Mr Pinto. Not yet,' she said curtly. 'Now listen to me. You were still in your chaddis when Bosco was the pride of Cavel. It still is. Your father Joseph, God praise his good soul, would swear by this, were he alive today. For years I have been asking you to register this property as heritage. But you don't care. You just don't. You are plain greedy and selfish, Mr Pinto.'

Ellena would have gone on had Shane not interjected, 'Ms Gomes, stop casting aspersions on him. He only has our interests at heart. If the building collapses, and Christ, it looks like it soon will, we all are going to go under. And you, Mr Coutinho and Mr Lawrence will be the ones to blame,' he said.

'Shane, shut up!' Michael barked. 'If you had such a huge problem with this building, why did you move here in the first place?'

'I agree,' Mario said. 'The Braganzas have no clue about the history of Bosco. It has reared several treasures. Bombay's famous D'Lima family, the most renowned architects, engineers, bakers, brave firefighters like my father and newspaper editors came from this building. It's a jewel in the crown of the city. You think we will allow it to disappear just like that?'

Neal listened patiently to all the arguments, his own vilification and the endless blame game. He had taken on the role of the moderator of a debate, feigning to be a neutral party, interrupting only to nudge one side or ask pointed questions and, most importantly, prevent any party from straying from the topic.

'Mrs da Cunha, you haven't spoken yet,' he said, when tempers had cooled and everyone was quiet.

She was a little low. Benji did not turn up for the meeting. He had promised he'd be present and help her make her point. Instead of him, she had the spirit of Joe sitting by her side and taunting her. 'Didn't I tell you this would happen, my sweet Anna?' she could hear him say. 'Your Benji has abandoned you.' His menacing laugh split her head.

'Are you okay?' Neal asked, noticing how disheartened she looked.

'I really have nothing to say,' Annette mumbled.

'What does that mean?' he enquired. 'Do you want to move or not?'

'Nothing matters anymore,' she replied.

Shane was mortified when he heard this. 'What are you saying?' he asked her angrily. 'It was you who pushed me to hold this meeting, and now you're telling us it doesn't matter. Such a waste of time, Mrs da Cunha.'

Neal was running out of patience. The residents of Lobo Mansion were very easy to please, but not this lot. Having already suffered enough humiliation at the hands of Ellena Gomes, who had taken a dig at him by harping on his dead father's competence, there was only one thing on his mind— he wanted to prove that he was just as honourable as his father. He closed the Bosco Mansion file that was sitting on his desk and said emphatically, 'Case closed then. You can all go back to your homes. Bosco is going nowhere for now.'

Shane, who had been following up on the issue indefatigably for a month, looked wistful. Annette put her head down, embarrassed that she had acted so thoughtlessly on the insistence of her useless husband.

'And what about the repairs?' Ellena asked as they all got up to leave.

'Yes, I was just going to discuss that,' Neal replied. He was lying. The thought had not come to him until Ellena had broached it. 'I will get an engineer to carry out a structural audit of the building soon. I can decide only after that. Until then, I would appreciate it if all the residents, especially those who no longer live in Bosco, stay on. If you want to save the building, you will have to be around to take care of it. Otherwise, all this big talk makes no sense.' He was pleased with his last jibe.

Ellena left the office soon after. She didn't wait to speak with Michael or Mario. By the time the two old men took the lift down, she had already left for home in a taxi.

'She could have given us a lift. What's this woman's problem?' Mario asked Michael.

'I am not going to complain, Mario. She saved us.'

'Aah! I see. Someone is impressed,' Mario teased. Michael ignored him.

This silence was long and painful. To be living so close to Ellena and then to see her behave like he didn't exist felt strange. In the few months since her return, their paths had crossed several times. In fact, every day in church. Michael wasn't a regular church-goer at all. But when he learnt from his sister that Ellena Gomes had started attending the 6.30 weekday mass in the mornings, he quietly followed suit.

'What's wrong with you, men?' Annette said when she saw her brother, who hated early mornings, leave home impeccably dressed at 6.15 a.m. He still had a decent mop of grey hair on his head and unlike many men his age, he hadn't needed to come to terms with a bald patch. Annette noticed him spending several minutes staring into the tiny mirror that was placed on the windowsill of his drawing room, sliding the teeth of his comb through his oiled hair till the strands had all slipped back. 'Joe is asking if you are going for mass or some fashion show? You are turning eighty this year, don't forget,' she joked. She went on, 'Benji also said something mean, but don't worry, I am not listening to him anymore. He's out of my life.'

Michael ignored all of them.

Michael was ignoring everybody these days. And Ellena was ignoring Michael.

In this game of ignoring and being ignored, the two found a silly comfort. He remained persistent and she adamant.

197

JANE BORGES

At mass, Michael would sit in the same pew as she did, hoping she'd at least turn to him when the priest asked the congregation to offer the sign of peace to each other. But she'd fold her hands and bow to everyone around her except him. There would be a moment when their eyes met, but she would make no effort to hold his gaze longer than a fraction of a second. But that moment was enough for Michael to get an eyeful.

Five years of living away from the city had done Ellena Gomes well. She still preferred only blue outfits but had switched to wearing loose pants and floral shirts. 'It's the magic of this new yoga class she is attending,' Annette had offhandedly mentioned to her brother one day. 'After all, you can't stretch in skirts.'

In church, she wore her hair—a striking balance of black and steely grey—in a tight bun on top of her head, which lifted her drooping cheeks. It was, however, her kohl-rimmed eyes hidden behind her glasses that took Michael some time getting used to. 'At seventy-six, who is she trying to please? Has she found herself a boyfriend in Goa?' he wondered. There wasn't a dearth of potential boyfriends. The singles, the retired and the widowed—they were all there, looking for new friends. As this thought came to his mind, he felt a tinge of jealousy shoot through him.

After mass ended, Ellena would walk home at such a quick pace that Michael would find himself panting halfway. He just couldn't keep up. He realised that to Ellena, he was just a ghost—both invisible and unwanted.

Two years was a long time to have waited to apologise, and Michael was aware of this. He had tried his best with his last letter, but then he wasn't sure why she was so upset with him. For not falling in love with her? Until she had written to him, he had not even known of Ellena's affection for him. And because she had been so good at keeping up the charade, there was no way that he could ever have found out otherwise.

What Michael didn't understand was that Ellena never wanted an apology. She didn't want him to fall in love with her either. She just wished he had acknowledged her feelings, and probably his own as well.

Ellena wasn't a romantic. Or rather, she had outgrown romance in the prime of her life. Her three relationships, all very brief, had drained her because she felt absolutely nothing for the men involved. 'I feel no music,' she had explained to her mum. After those failed attempts at falling in love, Ellena became fiercely protective of her heart; she could not let go of it anymore. But the ease with which her friendship with Michael blossomed when they had started writing to each other three years ago thawed her. Ellena was slowly able to let go—not just of her heart, but her entire self.

Their romance was in the tiny details, like the quarter and eighth notes of a musical composition that come softly but disappear even before you can linger in their sounds. But Michael was listening and even swaying to these notes. He latched onto Ellena's words, 'Go to church and talk to God'— she had not meant the advice to be taken literally, knowing very well that he was an agnostic, but he had. He read and re-read her letters because they made him smile and helped him fight the hours of loneliness. The effortless flirting was also the magic of this song.

Ellena, too, began singing the same tune. When Michael asked her to be more patient with her maid's kids, she gave them her all. Today, one of them was a school topper. When he nudged her to learn Konkani, she actually started going for professional classes—she hadn't told him about it. When he asked her to fly, she did come out of her cocoon. 'You are finally a butterfly,' he said.

This friendship had great potential. They would have done a lot of things that would have been good for each other. But perhaps it was a fear of putting a label on a relationship that wasn't a clear black and white, but a grey in-between, that made Michael nervous. Ellena's own insistence on testing new waters so suddenly led her to act impulsively. She used a full stop when a comma would have sufficed. The good thing is that the universe doesn't understand the rules of grammar. Punctuation isn't part of its lexicon.

The first week of June was aggressively warm and humid. Chira Bazaar no longer wore the sheen of summer. The gulmohar trees that grew between busy, broken pathways were axed to make way for larger buildings. The area had transformed in the short span of five years. Rows of tiny buildings and chawls were being demolished to make way for high-rises that popped up haphazardly.

As Ellena Gomes trundled through the bustling market stretch, she noticed that one such high-rise had already come up not very far from the eighty-three-year-old Vanguard Art and Photo Studio. The studio, she heard, was also going to bite the redevelopment bullet. Started in 1927 by an enterprising businessman named Jayantilal Chhabildas Morvi from Gujarat's Kathiawar, the studio had been the dugout of several prominent nationalist leaders, including Khan Abdul Ghaffar Khan and Babu Genu Said, Jawaharlal Nehru, his wife Kamla and daughter Indira Gandhi. Here was preserved a bit of these people to be revered later.

Ellena remembered her father telling her of the time when Subhash Chandra Bose visited the studio in 1930. When the locals heard that Bose was there, all of them, including her father, went in droves to catch a glimpse of him. 'Netaji ki jai,' they chanted until police officers cleared the crowd. An oil painting recreated from a photograph of Bose taken on that day, in which he was wearing traditional Bengali attire, now adorned the studio's interiors. Ellena couldn't believe that this two-thousand-square-foot vintage space that boasted mahogany wood cabins, antique light fittings and a hand-carved false ceiling—all of which she was once in awe of—would soon be a thing of the past.

It took her another twenty minutes to reach the fish market. Sunday mornings here were chaotic. The crowds were packed like sardines, struggling to navigate the sea of human bodies as they searched for their preferred fishmongers—the ones they could trust for a fine deal. It was surprising how easy it had become for Ellena to crawl through this bedlam. Earlier, when she lived in Mumbai, she was so unfit that it was difficult for her to just climb up and down her building stairs. But yoga had been kind to her body.

It had happened by accident. When her fixed deposits started depleting, Ellena rented out a room in her cottage in Goa to a Malayali yoga instructor, who wanted to hold classes there. The money was good and allowed her an occasional splurge. The icing on the cake was that she got to participate in the classes for free.

As soon as Ellena walked into the market, Pramila Gore, an old vendor, well-known in the area for the last forty-five years, called out to her excitedly from the stone parapet where she was sitting with the other fishmongers.

'*Aalana*, madam!' the Koli woman, who was more comfortable speaking in Marathi, yelled in broken Hindi. '*Kitna din hua?*'

Ellena smiled when she spotted the familiar face. '*Arre, hum* Goa *main tha.*'

'*Maloom hai, maloom hai* … Michael *saab ne bataya.*'

His name gave Ellena a feeling of discomfort, but she didn't show it.

'*Jhinga kaise diya?*' she asked.

'*Do-sau rupay ek kilo ka,* madam.'

'Two hundred rupees? Make it less. *Hum kitna purana* customer *hai.*'

'Madam, rain coming,' said another fisherwoman sitting beside Pramila, trying to meddle in the bargaining. 'All fish expensive now,' she rattled away in the little English that she knew.

'I don't buy any fish in the monsoon,' Ellena told the woman.

'Why, madam?'

'All very bad. Not fresh at all.'

'So what you eat whole baarish season, madam?'

'Prawn balchão,' said Ellena.

'Balchão?' the fishmonger asked, surprised. 'What this, madam?'

'It's a pickle. It's a delicious prawn pickle.'

The making of balchão was an annual monsoon ritual in the Gomes' kitchen. Ellena's mum Giselle had discouraged her kids from eating seafood during the rainy months of June and July, as it was the breeding season for most fish. Since fishing was restricted for the same reason, Giselle Gomes suspected that the catch available in the markets was either frozen or stale.

'It's unhealthy,' she'd tell Ellena. 'Not good for your stomach.'

While prawn balchão was a popular side dish—the making of which the Goans learned from their Portuguese brethren—Giselle reinvented her fish pickles with balchão masala.

Just a week or two before the monsoon, which usually began in mid-June, Ellena's mother would buy a large stock of prawns from the market. The very same day, she'd get started—first cleaning and deveining the prawns, and then marinating them. The pickle would be ready by evening and stored in a ceramic jar.

It would be their go-to dish for seafood over the next few months, enjoyed with dal and rice, or simply relished between slices of bread. 'Mama, this is so delicious,' Ellena would say each time she bit into the sweet-pungent prawn.

After Giselle passed away, Ellena once attempted to make prawn balchão from the hand-written recipe book—a family heirloom, which had meticulous notes by her mum and nana. But Ellena couldn't rustle up a meal to save her life. She gave up after that first attempt, and stopped eating seafood completely during the rainy season.

In Goa, though, there had been so much time at hand that she was forced to nurture unknown interests—cooking, for instance. She began with cutlets before trying her hand at fish curries, including the tangy ambotik, and her mum's peas pulao and vindaloo. Her maid, Lorna, was always around to offer a hand and free advice, if and when she struggled. Ellena, however, experienced a string of bad luck when preparing balchão. The first batch came out very spicy. 'You didn't pick the right chillies,' her maid told her.

The following year, the pickle didn't last even two days. 'Did you add water while grinding the masalas?' her maid asked. When Ellena nodded, the amused maid slapped her forehead. 'Kitté re aunty. You should only add vinegar. Water will kill your pickle.'

Unfortunately, in her next attempt, Ellena was more than generous with the vinegar, and the balchão turned sour.

'Where is your heart?' Lorna asked. Ellena looked at her, confused. 'Oho aunty, bring some love into your cooking … mog kar,' the maid suggested with a smile.

When Ellena arrived in the compound of Pope's Colony with the bag of fresh prawns, it was already 11.30 a.m. Mario and Michael were outside, sitting on a wooden bench that the two had recently invested in, so that the latter could spend some time away from Annette and her ghosts. Since walking two floors up to Mario's house daily was getting incredibly difficult for Michael these days, they had settled for Michael's front garden. The bench was placed beneath a canopy made of wooden sticks, which had several climbing vine plants growing above and under it—ingeniously designed by Merlyn several years ago.

'Taking a stroll in the morning sun, are you?' Mario asked when Ellena got to the building.

'Yes,' she said, trying to avoid small talk.

He could smell the salt of the sea in her bag. 'Aha! You went to the fish market.'

'Yes,' she said again. Michael sat quietly, looking the other way, trying to show no interest in this conversation.

'What did you get?' Mario prodded.

'Mario, I am sorry, but you must excuse me. I am really tired,' Ellena said and took the stairs.

'Seriously, what's her problem?' Mario asked Michael when she had left. 'She is treating us like rats. What have we done? Tell me, is she still angry with you for getting that pipeline? That would be very petty.'

'I don't think so,' Michael said.

'Then what! I would have understood if she treated Shane or Annette the same way, but she talks to them so nicely. What have we done?'

'It's me, not you.'

After returning to Bombay, it took Ellena days to get her kitchen in order. In the beginning, she showed no inclination to stay here. Pernem was so comfortable and peaceful, she did not want to be anywhere else. But following the structural audit last month, the landlord announced that the building would be repaired sometime after the monsoon and that the residents would need to be around. The auditor noticed some major cracks on the top floors; the putty too had fallen out in chunks in several places. 'The building needs to be repaired on an urgent basis,' the auditor told the landlord. There was no telling how long it would take. But given the age of the structure, repairs were going to be slow. 'You will all have to be patient,' Neal told the residents.

Since Mario had a freelance job and could work out of any city, the shift didn't hit him much. His new girlfriend had apparently left him too, so nobody would be missing him back in London. Michael was slowly growing wary of some of Mario's stories of the high life. It wasn't that he didn't believe Mario, but the exaggerations were too hard to ignore.

But Ellena wasn't happy with the development. It would mean socialising more often with the folks in Cavel, and while she had loved engaging in unwanted chit-chat at one point in time, she had zero threshold for it now. Her most imminent concern, however, was the dearth of blue dresses and pants in her wardrobe—she hadn't carried enough for this extended stay. When she resigned herself to her old life at Bosco, she sent money to Lorna, requesting her to ship a carton with all her clothes to Mumbai. To her tenant, the yoga instructor from Kerala, who had also taught Ellena how to line her eyes, she wrote saying that she could have the entire cottage for a year at least, for a very small increase in rent.

Her kitchen in Goa boasted every kind of appliance and tool, and was always well-stocked—a reflection of how much she cooked. The one in Mumbai was basic. It harked back to a time when she only knew how to make eggs and tea. The newly purchased bottles of whole spices and ground masalas were placed inside a broken cabinet. Apart from this, there was an old single stove, a grinder, and a mini Godrej refrigerator that she had bought around fifteen years ago, which had only enough place to store her veggies and fruits.

Sundays at home were lazy and quiet, like any other day. Except that, Ellena's best friend, Joana, who lived in the neighbourhood, would drop by for tea in the late afternoons.

Ellena wanted to finish making the balchão before Joana visited and ambushed her with gossip.

She placed the prawns in a glass bowl and rinsed them thoroughly in warm water. She then pulled up a wooden stool and, sitting on it, quietly worked her way through each prawn, undressing it between her thin, shrivelled fingers; first twisting its head and plucking it off, then placing her right thumb beneath the prawn to peel off the shell gently, before sliding her knife through the top of its slimy surface to clean out the gooey black vein.

Ellena held the naked prawn between her fingers, its flesh soft and translucent pink. This was her now, after all those years of hopelessly loving, pining, seething and hurting. The wall she had built around herself was slowly falling apart, exposing her to herself.

An hour later, when she had finally completed the chore, a mound of hollow shells with pairs of black peppercorn eyes and loosely hanging antennae sat on an old newspaper. She folded the edges of the paper carefully, ensuring that all the waste she had collected was firmly locked in. Lifting herself off the stool, she reached for the plate of cleaned prawns and wrapped them in a kitchen towel to soak up all the excess water, before letting the prawns settle in a marinade of turmeric and salt.

'When you rub salt into an open wound, it's likely to singe, but turmeric has a cooling effect. That's why we always use them together,' Ellena recalled her mum telling her when she had enquired why Giselle used the same marinade for all meat and fish. Her mum continued, 'The salt and haldi will let the fish heal. It needs to heal, otherwise eating it won't make you happy. How can you enjoy something that still holds a grudge against you for having killed it?'

Ellena deep-fried her prawns in oil and removed them when they were crunchy and golden brown. She then took a fistful of dried Kashmiri chillies—carefully hand-picked from the bazaar as Lorna had advised, to give the perfect combination of flavour and colour to the pickle—and put it in the grinder. She added cumin, a dash of red chilli powder, peppercorns, cloves, cinnamon sticks, soaked tamarind, whole garlic cloves and diced ginger, mixing it all with copious amounts of vinegar to make a thick paste.

'Each time you prepare the balchão masala, think of the person you want to feed it to. If it's someone you dislike, you might end up being too liberal with your spices. If this person is somebody you love, you will be more careful, especially with your peppercorns and chillies. You don't want to burn the tongue that has been kind to you,' Lorna had advised in Konkani.

The pan sizzled as Ellena poured the oil, rather too generously. 'The balchão needs the oil, because it's a pickle,' her mum had said when Ellena raised a stink about the amount of oil she was adding. 'Why do you worry about the oil? Pickles are anyway supposed to be relished only in small portions. Life is like that, my baby. The best part cannot be enjoyed whole, or it will become too much for you to digest.'

When the oil was hot enough, she added mustard seeds, curry leaves, and some more garlic and ginger, sautéing them till the masala became a golden brown. She transferred the ground masala into the pan and added salt and a teaspoon of sugar, mixing it all.

'How is it that the balchão lasts so long, mama?' Ellena had asked.

'It's the vinegar. It not only adds a sharp flavour to the pickle but is also a natural preservative. It will keep your balchão forever.'

'But no food can last forever, mama,' Ellena had exclaimed.

'Nothing lasts forever, baby, but it also depends on what your forever is. Is it a day? Is it a month? Is it a year? We make our own forevers.'

When the pungent smell of the masala wafted through the kitchen, Ellena added the prawns, tossing them well till they were cooked. She turned off the gas, and let the pan cool. That's when her doorbell rang.

The evening passed surprisingly fast. Joana didn't indulge in too much nonsense talk today and was discussing plans of moving back to Goa by the end of next year.

'Our lovely old Bombay has gone to the dogs,' she said. 'What a tragedy this place has become. Construction everywhere, so much traffic, and the pollution is unbearable.'

'I never liked Bombay either, Jo. But when I first moved to Pernem, I used to miss Cavel a lot,' Ellena said.

'Really?'

'Yes. But what I realised after staying away from Cavel all these years is that you end up taking a part of this place with you wherever you go. And then you start another Cavel in your new home.'

'Uhh! I don't quite understand what you mean, Elle,' Joana said, confused.

'Well, Cavel is not just a place, it's also the sum total of its people and their experiences,' Ellena said. 'And because its people are everywhere, Cavel is everywhere.'

After Joana left, Ellena went back to the kitchen and checked on her balchão. It was a fiery red. The pickle would taste best after it had matured over a few weeks, but it looked too delicious to resist. She took out a tasting spoon from her kitchen drawer and dipped it into the thick masala, scooping out a very small portion. Ellena Gomes allowed her tongue to savour every bit of it.

It was half past nine in the evening when Michael heard a faint knock on his door. It was so light that if the trees hadn't been so still outside, he would probably have missed it altogether. Annette had hit the sack early today. He was glad, because it gave him some time to concentrate on other things.

When he opened the door, he found Mario, as expected, standing outside. This was a weekend routine.

'Care for a drink in the garden?' Mario asked, flashing a thermos. Mario's idea of a drink was a good cup of hot coffee, since he had never warmed to the bottle. 'I've got some chakna too,' he said, pulling out a packet of peanuts from a plastic bag. 'Freshly roasted.'

'Ugh! I am not so sure, Mario. I have to send this column tonight. It's a bit urgent,' Michael said. 'But you can come in, I will give you company.'

'Naa. Not with your sister around. Let's drink tomorrow instead?'

Michael had already known what Mario's response was going to be. He would do anything to stay away from Michael's home, especially after a major tiff with Annette some weeks ago.

'Sure. That sounds good to me,' Michael replied.

On any another day, Michael would have told Mario that they could enjoy their coffee and chakna at home as Annette was fast asleep, but not today. He shut the door behind Mario and went back to the dining table, where he had just served himself dinner.

Michael tore off a piece of pao and slathered it liberally with the dollop of thick gravy that only a few minutes ago he had spooned out of a glass jar. He put the bread in his mouth and chewed it slowly—the juice of the ground spices bursting inside him, spinning his head into a slow whirl.

He could feel his feet move lithely on the ground, her feet following swiftly behind him. The two of them were running, chasing each other from one tree to another building, negotiating tiny pebbles, fallen half-eaten mangoes, broken bark, slippery ground moss and brown puddles, until a cul-de-sac broke their game. He stopped. She stopped, and her hands gently tapped his shoulders. 'Caught you,' she said and giggled like a little girl.

But when he turned around, everything was a blur except for the glass jar she was holding. He reached for it, opened the jar and dug out a prawn. He bit into its flesh, licking the cooked, ground spices smeared between his fingers. A tear trickled down his face. His balchão tasted of pure love.

EPILOGUE

Ellena Gomes,
Casa Gomes, Socoillo Waddo,
Pernem, Goa

2 January 2010

Hi Ellena,

I am not sure how to begin this letter, so I will start by asking you the obvious: how are you? It has been a long time, yes. And I have no excuse for not writing back. I wouldn't be lying if I said that I had tried writing once. But I gave up. I couldn't handle it. I feared you would burn my letter again.

Over the last two years, I have introspected often about everything we shared in those letters. I can't speak for you, but I will for myself. I was so happy just writing to you and hearing from you that I hadn't noticed where all of this was heading. When I did, I think I panicked. It wasn't the right time for me to make sense of anything.

I had just lost my wife, and I had just won a new friend. I should have been grateful, but I wasn't. First I said the wrong things, and then I remained silent for a very long time. In the process, I hurt you badly. I am sorry. I am really very sorry.

Ellena, I want to begin with you again. I cannot promise a whole lot of things, especially love, of which at this age I have become so wary. But this world is full of possibilities. If nothing else, I will have won myself a best friend. Do tell me if I can come and visit you.

Yours truly,
Michael Coutinho

ACKNOWLEDGEMENTS

Cavel is as real as it has been imagined. My familiarity with the sights and sounds of this South Mumbai neighbourhood shaped this novel in more ways than one. It would, however, be a lie to say that the inspiration ended there. Its residents are gifted storytellers, and sometimes, knowingly and even unknowingly, they shared snatches of their memories around which I wove my fiction. The stories began with Lulu Days in 2005—she passed away last year, at 102—and continued with my dearest friend and veteran journalist, the late Ervell E. Menezes, whose honest review of one of my initial drafts made me rethink the entire project.

This book also owes a lot to my aunt Vivienne Gaudet, a former hockey player for India, who now resides in Canada. When I reached out to her for help, she readily parted with her memoir, meant only for her son (my cousin) and granddaughter. It had beautiful and bitter-sweet moments from Cavel, where she spent her childhood and youth. My handsome uncle Patrick Crasto, who once lived there, shared many amusing vignettes too. I'd also like to thank noted fashion designer and Khotachi Wadi resident James Ferreira for welcoming me to his gorgeous home on several occasions and introducing me to his lovely neighbours. All these interactions helped me place my fictitious characters and events in a world that had some semblance of reality. Here, I can't forget to mention my grandmother Anna Borges, who grew up in a Christian pocket in Mazagaon. Even though mai's mind plays tricks on her these days, she continues to be a delicious raconteur.

Historicising some parts of the text also meant getting the facts right. I read late historian Teresa Albuquerque's *Goan Pioneers in Bombay* to understand the migration of Goans to Bombay, the proliferation of Christian hamlets in the city and the medical genius that was Dr Acacio Gabriel Viegas. A careful reading of fashion designer Wendell Rodricks' book *Moda Goa: History and Style* gave me a sense of Goan fashion. Jerry Pinto's piece, 'The Day it Rained Gold Bricks and a Horse Ran Headless', from the book *Bombay, Meri Jaan: Writings on Mumbai*, was also part of my reading material to get timelines right for the story. Noted Mumbai Police historian Deepak Rao helped throw light on Prohibition in Bombay and Dr Fleur D'Souza, former HOD of History at St Xavier's College, took time out of her busy schedule one evening, to have an extended telephonic chat on East Indian history. Over a series of text messages, historian and author Dr Fatima da Silva Gracias explained the shared histories of Goans and Mangaloreans. I also reached out to chef and author Floyd Cardoz, who wrote to me about balchão— he described the preserve as a 'pickle-like dish that is the pride of most Goans'—and how much he relished it as a child. US-based Xanti Pinto, who runs the recipe blog Xantilicious, shared essential tips for preparing the prawn balchão pickle. Covering heritage and urban planning for the *Sunday mid-day* in Mumbai brought me closer to many hidden stories and gems from the city that I wasn't aware of, and of which you will find traces in my narrative.

A lot of friends also showed immense faith in this book, when I had none. I'd like to begin with Arundhati Pattabhiraman, who has been the force behind this novel. She read and re-read every draft from the day I started writing it. Tess Joss, Dylan D'Silva and N.S. Abhayakumar read the entire draft in record time and gave valuable feedback. Sajini Sahadevan, Sébastien Lemaire, Sohini Mitter, Blessy Chettiar, Candice Martins, Nishath Nizar and Kusumita Das had some kind words and constructive feedback on chapters they read. To all of them, a big thank you.

No success is complete without family. I started writing this book in 2015, when I briefly moved to Muscat and was living with my dad, Johnny Borges. There were days when I wrote ferociously. During this time, it was his silence that ensured I never lost rhythm. My mamma, Sandra, who makes the best coffee in the world, made sure that I got enough of it when I woke up during odd hours to write. My brother Saby and she have also been subjected to some terrible drafts, and they've rarely complained. Steven, my youngest brother, has brainstormed everything from the characters to the title of the book, and to him I owe its completion.

Finally, I would like to thank my literary agent, Anish Chandy of Labyrinth Literary Agency, for showing confidence in a shelved project. And most importantly, team Westland—my commissioning editor, Sanghamitra Biswas, for her vision for this book and my publisher, Karthika VK. She is an institution, and I have had the good fortune of working with her.

There are also some amazing mentors, colleagues and friends who I am blessed to have in my life. If I have missed names, I promise to make up for it in person.